THE CHALICE

MW01147996

Book Two

THE CROWN OF
THE CRESCENT MOON

by

C. K. Sholly

Warbler Press

WP

The Chalice Rose Series

Book I The Sword Argente
Book II The Crown of the Crescent Moon
Book III The Chalice Rose

Dedicated to all the denizens of the waters

Far in the north of Kepler186f where polar ice caps creep southward in winter, the small continent of Allanda thrives in the caress of a warm sea current from the south. Twice the inhabitants were nearly obliterated by a combination of disease, war, and sudden climate changes. Those who survived remembered nothing of their origins.

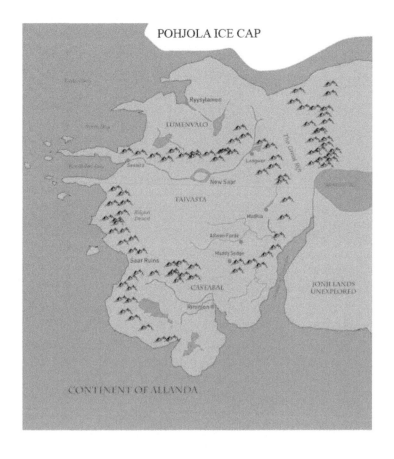

Table of Contents

Chapter 1

TIME TO LEAVE

"Great deeds and bad news travel on swift wings."

-TAIVASTAN FOLK SAYING

I have to get up, Greylin thought. *Up...now. I can do this.*

She groaned as she sat up in bed. Every muscle in her body hurt and in spite of a long bath, she still reeked from contact with the giant sea monster she had killed the night before. Added to her discomfort was the fact that she had gotten little sleep; she had drifted off in the tub and woken up later, cold and wet. By then she was chilled through, so when she got into bed, she tossed and turned and finally gave up once the sun rose. Contributing to that problem was the fact that she was naked. She had thrown her clothes into an odorous pile as far away from her as she could get it, and her nakedness made her feel vulnerable and exposed even though she was alone in her room.

She braced herself to stand up and realized that she couldn't leave her room anyway because she had nothing to wear! She eyed the filthy pile of clothes stained with the blood and gore that she washed off her body earlier. The smell would never come off them, and the thought of putting them back on nearly made her retch.

She sighed with regret for the Mazarine cadet blues that had been stolen yesterday as part of a spell to trick her friends into chasing after an impostor. All she had left was a ripped dress and an extra tunic she had outgrown, one which she'd brought with her "just in case" when she left her home in Maddy Sedge. She pulled it out of her old rucksack and was hit with memories when the smell of home drifted to her. A wave of homesickness overwhelmed her, and she sat cross-legged in the middle of the bed, head in hands, fighting back tears. Too much had happened too quickly. It had been three months since she was attacked by a pack of slinkhounds and a dark shadow, three months on the road with the paladin Reist D'Arcannon and the mage Heron Hollinghast. She hardly knew who she was anymore.

A knock at the door startled her. "Yes?" she said, lifting her head.

"I have somet'ing for you, Lady."

Greylin recognized the voice of one of the serving maids from the Seal and Sailor Inn where she was staying. *Lady?* She thought, *They're calling me "lady" now?* She groaned in disbelief. Her secret was out; everyone knew she was not the farm boy she had been pretending to be.

"One moment."

She stood up, looked around, grabbed the thin blanket off the bed and wrapped it around her before she opened the door a crack and peered out suspiciously. Instead of a pack of thugs waiting to push their way through and capture her like they had tried to last night, there was only Dina the chambermaid—she thought that was her name. Dina had a speech problem, and Greylin couldn't tell if she had said Tina, Dina or Gina—waiting on the other side of the door with piles of fabric in her arms. She curtsied.

"Lady, t'ese were brought over by t'at boy, Finn." It came out sounding like "Vtfinn" when she said it. "He said you might need t'em."

Greylin tucked the blanket under her arms and took the pile. It was comprised of two sets of Sessirran clothes: rough-cut, tea-dyed, loose sailor shorts and half-sleeve shirts that all the Sessirran men and women wore. Her eyes filled with tears of gratitude. *I must still be rattled from everything that happened last night. I'm overly emotional.* She tried to shake it off but instead, a tear fell down her cheek even as she smiled at the fact that he had sent such a thoughtful gift. *This tells me he forgives me my deception of being a boy. Maybe...though both men and women wear these outfits. Lucky for him. He can't lose,* she thought, smiling through her tears.

"Thank you," she breathed as she grabbed the clothes with one hand and clutched them to her. One problem solved, she thought. "Oh, wait," she said and ran over to her rucksack and took out a coin for Dina. The girl beamed like the morning sun, curtsied, and took her leave. Greylin closed the door gently.

Finn was Greylin's Sessirran friend, a Selkan she had met only a week ago. Selkans were a seal-like people who lived side-by-side with humans in the beautiful port city of Sessirra. Finn had been with her last night when she was lured to the other side of Pearladen Bay by a gang of thugs determined to kidnap her. She and Finn were tricked by a note left in her friends' room telling them that Hollinghast and D'Arcannon were in trouble. *I should have known better!* she thought. It almost worked and would have if it hadn't been for Finn's strength and agility, and her discovery of the Eversilver Sword.

She reached for the sword now and held it close. She hated to have it out of her hand. Last night she didn't have good light to examine it. Now she scrutinized it in close detail in the morning sun: the runes, the precious stones embedded in the hilt, and the sturdy handguard. It was weighted perfectly and quivered with power. She had yearned for it from the first night she dreamt of it as a child, so long ago. She turned it in her hand, *this one perfect sword.* It had called to her and plagued her with longing for it.

Her two companions, the Master Mage Heron Hollinghast and the Paladin Reist D'Arcannon, were puzzled that she showed such great interest in a sword and so little interest in meeting the man who was possibly her father, King Sterren of Taivasta, but he didn't seem real to her, nor did she have any interest in attaining a position of power as the rightful heir.

If she had been asked what she truly wanted, she would have only described the sword she now held in her hand. Unfortunately, when she pulled the sword out of its ingenious hiding place, she inadvertently let the monster known as the Oarman out of his domain in the bay north of Sessirra. The sword had formed part of the intricate scrollwork on the lock that held the doors to the North Bay shut. His escape led to a frantic battle, one that she was only able to win because of the extraordinary properties of the sword itself.

She dressed as quickly as her sore muscles allowed, gritting her teeth and stifling groans. There was no way for her to wear the sword, she had no scabbard or belt, but she wasn't about to leave it in her room. She would just have to carry it. She eased herself downstairs in search of her two companions and one of the excellent breakfasts the kitchen of the Seal and Sailor Inn provided for its guests.

They were sitting at their usual table. Hollinghast was always the first to gain anyone's attention. Tall and thin and pale, he had "lightened" over time because of his practice of magic and dominated the room. His hair, which he wore caught in a silver clasp at the nape of his neck, had also faded from brown to white and glistened like snow in the morning sunlight. He turned his gentle, ice blue eyes toward Greylin and smiled with kindness, though she knew those eyes were full of magic and could pin her like a gimlet if she did something wrong. A white beard that was trimmed to the length of half a hand gave him an air of distinction which belied his youthful appearance.

D'Arcannon by contrast was strongly built and not as tall. He was from the tribal families of Langwer and claimed descent from both the Red Deer and Tarora Haka clans. He was deeply tanned with straight black hair that he trimmed to half a finger-width to prevent an opponent gaining advantage in a fight. Overshadowed at first by

Hollinghast's pristine white hair and robes, it wasn't until you noted the fine, high cheekbones on his clean-shaven face that you realized he was also a scene-stealer. It was his eyes, though, that attracted the most notice, especially from women, wherever he went. They were more than merely appealing; they smoldered with charisma, an attribute he seemed unaware of just as he seemed to be unaware of the female attention he garnered. It has been said that a paladin "only loves his horse and ELIEL". If Reist was to fall in love he would lose his ability to detect evil and cease to be a paladin, and that was a role he valued above all else.

As she entered the dining room, she noticed a line of Sessirran dignitaries waiting near the entrance from the street, and hoped they had nothing to do with her. While she understood the appreciation the Sessirran citizens must feel toward her, she was tired and sore and wanted to be left alone. She slipped quietly into the common room and sat down in her usual chair next to her friends. The two men glanced at her appearance, raised their eyebrows, looked at each other, then sat back and looked at her for an explanation.

"Finn sent them over," she explained in a matter-of-fact tone.

"Superb!" Hollinghast exclaimed in his usual enthusiastic good humor that was almost too much to bear first thing in the morning. "I was wondering what we were going to do about that. We were just discussing it in fact. We'd thought you'd sleep a little longer. D'Arcannon was going to see if he could get another set of blues from the Mazarine Hall, but this is even better! You'll blend right in."

This was immediately proved wrong by the line of Sessirrans who were hesitantly approaching to pay their respects. They had no problem recognizing her at all. She had been taking a chance masquerading as a boy. That sort of thing was frowned on, and if the priests had their way with her, she might have been branded with an "F" and cast out on the streets to beg, but fame had its advantages.

"From the looks of things, it's time to leave," D'Arcannon muttered under his breath as he looked at the line of well-wishers.

"I've been thinking about that," Hollinghast replied in an undertone. "I think our best bet would be to travel by sea to Lumenvalo. Any other direction will be too dangerous once word of all this gets out. Any overland travel will be easily tracked."

The first well-wisher turned out to be Mayor-Council Môr Perlog. He approached, bowed, and held out a dazzling leather belt and scabbard, dyed gold and wrapped with fine metallic gold and eversilver threads. In spite of the fact that Greylin didn't want a lot of bother made over the events of the night before, she did need the scabbard. Carrying the sword around loose was clumsy, dangerous, and awkward. The Mayor-Council explained that the scabbard had been on display at the Merchants Hall for centuries waiting for its rightful owner to appear. He seemed to think this was Greylin, and she wasn't going to argue. Though he pleaded for a formal ceremony, Hollinghast indicated that they couldn't stay, so they compromised by awarding it to her now.

There was a lot of clapping and cheering which made Greylin want to hide or run, but she had to settle for flushing a vivid pink. Thankfully, the Innkeeper— Burleigh by name—arrived with breakfast for all. He brought out fresh hot loaves of spiced bread that smelled deliciously mouth-watering, some crispy-fried *fisal* fish, bacon, and separate plates of poached eggs.

Greylin was so hungry she thought she might eat all of it herself. Luckily, he brought seconds and thirds because everyone seemed to have huge appetites after the previous night's excitement. Mercifully, the Sessirrans were eating at other tables at a discreet distance, and Greylin was allowed to eat in peace. They could hear the conversation from the surrounding tables, and it was clear the Sessirrans were going to waste no time in opening up the North Bay for settlement and trade.

Chapter 2

TO LUMENVALO

"Lumenvalo is a haven of delight in the summer.
In the winter it is a nightmare of darkness and snow."

- THE TRAVELS OF KING ARDEON OF CASTABAL

Hollinghast went to settle the bill with Innkeeper Burleigh and the two of them got into a lengthy conversation. Greylin thought she heard "ship" and "Lumenvalo" as she and D'Arcannon took their leave of the crowded dining hall and went upstairs to retrieve their belongings and headed out to the stables. D'Arcannon saddled Bane, his big Midnight Friesian—glossy, powerful, and impatient—who hadn't taken a liking to the stable boy. Hollinghast's mare, a cream-colored, curly-maned mare who was as leggy as the wizard, was the opposite in temperament; she behaved like a lady wherever she was, and the stable boy attended to her.

Greylin saddled her own beloved Roki, the stallion she had rescued in the desert from groundmites that were venomous, man-sized lizards that rarely went after prey as large as horses unless they could trap them and wear them down. They had tried to do just that in a muddy spring that was set deep in a rock canyon. After she and her companions killed the horrid beasts, the stallion leading the small herd became smitten with Greylin and followed her everywhere. When she cleaned the mud off him, she discovered that his coat was bluish gray with pale white and dark dapples. D'Arcannon told her the stallion was a rare Leopard Horse, sometimes called a Fells Horse or Fell Pony. His mane and tail were a deep black like the shadows on the craggy fells of Langwer where they were sometimes seen. The Kilgari, the people of the desert, called him *Röyhkeä Varas* meaning "brazen thief" because he would steal their horses and always get away with it. They were happy to see him go. She shortened his name to "Roki", and they had been constant companions ever since. These days in the city had been hard on him, and though she visited him and rode a bit every day, it was not the same as the desert. He was restless and annoyed.

Greylin placed and smoothed the woven blanket on Roki's back that the Owda—the holy woman of the Kilgari—had gifted her with and which declared her to be a friend to the Kilgari. She was suddenly overwhelmed with fatigue and thought she might fall asleep standing up. The breakfast had done the trick, but now there was no time to sleep. She sighed and leaned against Roki's side. She should have tried to get something from the kitchen last night; it might have settled her down. Too late now. *Oh wait,* she realized—*I had no clothes then!* She pictured herself sneaking around naked trying to snatch a loaf of bread from the larder without being seen or caught—which St. Rauna only knows would have happened for sure. The thought made her laugh and Roki snorted.

There were also two mules that had accompanied them on their journey to carry their packs. Hollinghast joined them and after much discussion, they decided to leave them at the Mazarine Hall to be brought back to New Saar on their next routine change of guard. D'Arcannon flagged down two Mazarines who happened, luckily, to be passing by just then on patrol. He sent a message with them to Commander Rufter to report that he was leaving for Lumenvalo and requested to have the mules picked up at the Inn. Three horses and two mules would require a ship too large for them to hire on short notice. Greylin was sad to leave Patch; the mule was her first mount on the journey that had brought her here. Patch, on the other hand, remained unperturbed as always. They would have to leave a lot of gear behind as well but planned on purchasing new pack mounts and more gear once they got to Lumenvalo.

At last, they mounted to leave. Hollinghast turned to her with a smile and asked, "Would you like to say goodbye to Finn?"

Greylin's eyes filled with sudden tears again. Finn was a true friend. Her Aunt Daara, the woman who had kidnapped her as a child and raised her always kept her away from anyone who might get too close and find out the "secret" that she was really a girl, and possibly the deeper secret that she was the missing daughter of King Sterren Hilde. Greylin herself didn't know the truth of it. Even though Daara had finally admitted it to her two companions, the ultimate proof was that if she was truly a Hilde, she should have a birthmark, the *malja ruusu*, and she didn't.

Daara wanted to keep her safe and thought she had been successful until slinkhounds sniffed Greylin out a few months ago. If it hadn't been for Hollinghast's and D'Arcannon's intervention, Greylin would probably be dead by now. They had trailed the pack and arrived just in time. The slinkhounds went by scent. They didn't care if she had the birthmark or not, so Greylin wondered, *am I Sterren's daughter or not?*

Horses saddled and messages sent, the three headed out along the white cobblestone road turning down to the shoreline where Finn's home sat on the south shore of Pearladen Bay where many of the Selkan people lived.

"Thank you for letting me see Finn before we leave," Greylin said to her companions.

Greylin had met Finn the first day she arrived as she walked along the shore, marveling at the sights and smells of the ocean. He was a bit of an outcast because he had no love for ships and seafaring which was the heart and soul of the Selkans. Their seal-like characteristics of webbed fingers and toes, an extra eyelid to see clearly underwater, and their ability to hold their breath for minutes at a time allowed them to gather beautiful pearls treasured throughout the world. They had a strong relationship with the denizens of the sea: the seals, whale leviathans, and other sea mammals that helped them fish, navigate, and sometimes power and steer their boats when necessary.

She would miss the sounds of the seaport. Already people were calling to each other, wagons were rattling down to the docks, and gulls were screeching raucously overhead as the three companions rode along the road that skirted the bay. As she passed the boats and ships moored in the harbor, she gazed once more in fascination at the large curved outriggers, now locked in upright positions, that would allow whales to come up underneath and guide the ships to safety if need be. *How can a fish be that big?* she wondered. *Not a fish,* Finn would say. *They breathe air like we do.*

Finn was sitting outside his house mending nets. She jumped down from Roki and ran over to him to give him a hug.

"Thank you for the clothes!" she said.

"You're welcome," he said and laughed. "Look at you now. A real sailor."

"Whatever made you think of it?"

"I saw what happened to your clothes after that battle. I knew you'd need something and that it wouldn't occur to anyone else now that they had their 'Golden Pearl'. And if it did, they'd try to dress you up all girly. I didn't think you would like that."

"Golden Pearl!" Greylin snorted and laughed, which made them both laugh.

"It makes for a better legend than 'The Girl Covered in Goo'. Though you did sort of glow, you know," he continued. "I think your friend did something. All of a sudden you looked more like a lady in a long dress and your clothes seemed to shimmer." He looked down with sudden embarrassment. He was having a hard time getting used to the fact that she was a girl and now looked like one.

"I'm sorry I never told you I was really a girl," her voice dropped to a whisper. "And now I have to leave. There are people after me, like they were last night."

Finn nodded to Hollinghast and D'Arcannon waiting patiently a few yards behind.

"Where are you going?" he asked Greylin.

"Lumenvalo they said. By ship!" Greylin said as she turned to look over her shoulder at her companions.

"Let me talk to them a moment," Finn said, putting his net to one side. "Stay here."

Chapter 3

CASTING OFF

*"Never expect children to choose to be with
anyone but their friends."*

- Father Jacob from *Twenty Years of
Wisdom from the Orphan House*

She stood there a moment and then wondered why she
was standing there. Hearing the discussion wasn't going to
make a difference was it? Would Finn have said that if he
didn't know she was a girl?

Finn and Hollinghast talked, pointed a bit, and
Hollinghast dismounted. While all this was going on,
Greylin noticed that people were starting to stop and stare
at her instead of going about their business. *I'm attracting
a crowd,* she thought. *Better that I do stay over here… then
they won't notice what's going on over there.* She tried to
smile nicely but not encourage them all to approach her.
She was unsuccessful; they smiled back and started edging
closer.

"Thank you, Lady," one woman said sweetly as she
touched her hand. Soon they were all touching and
thanking her, and generally making her uncomfortable.
Sessirrans were a superstitious lot, and she had a feeling
that touching her was considered good luck. She tried to
be gracious and not panic as she looked over at the
discussion which seemed to finally be winding up. Finn
came back and asked if he could ride with her. She asked
Roki and got a mental picture of the two of them riding
him.

"I'll be right back," Finn called over his shoulder as he
ran into the house. She mounted and the people who had

gathered around her backed off a bit, shy of the horse. *I should have thought of that earlier!* Roki shivered all over and snorted which pushed them back even more. *Good boy,* she thought.

In a few moments Finn returned with a cloth bag and jumped up behind her. His mother came out to watch. Like all Selkans, she had light, sand-colored hair and darker skin. She was wearing one of the many-pocketed aprons Selkan women wore to keep their tools at their fingertips. She waved good-bye and her look of pride declared to everyone that she was no longer the mother of a misfit who wouldn't go out to sea, but the mother of the Golden Pearl's friend.

"Where are we going?" Greylin asked as Roki began to move forward.

"All the way down to the end dock," Finn replied, pointing ahead.

"What's in the bag?" she asked.

"Extra clothes. Odds and ends. I'm coming with you."

"What?" She turned and tried to look him in the eye.

He laughed. "We're going on my cousin's ship the *Windracer*. It can take us all, including the horses. He was going north anyway and didn't have a full cargo."

Greylin's heart leaped for joy. Suddenly everything was an adventure again. She was puzzled though, "You can leave? Just like that?"

"Most boys my age have already gone to sea. I was hanging about because I didn't want to. I can leave whenever I want, I should be on a Selkan Searun anyway—should have been a year ago—which is when a young man leaves to make his way in the world. With us it's usually by signing on to crew a ship but going with all of you will suit just fine. Even my Ma feels it's time for me to move along with life even though she'll miss me. My brothers and sisters will be thrilled, though, when they find out."

"I didn't know you had any brothers and sisters!"

"Oh aye, they're all out to sea, most of them married."

"Your father..." she trailed off and wasn't sure how to ask.

"Oh aye, I had one," he snickered. "Did you wonder? Lost at sea he was." He shrugged, "It happens."

Greylin pondered that as they pulled up at the last dock. She liked the look of the *Windracer* immediately. She was a wide, sturdy ship with what Finn described as a "low draft" and could sail far up a river without hitting bottom. The prow was carved into a horse's head which she took to be a good omen. Finn ran up the gangplank and began talking animatedly to another Selkan she took to be his cousin. After much gesturing, he returned and gave the go ahead to board.

They dismounted and led their horses up the gangplank. She caught a glint of gold or silver passing into the captain's hand from Hollinghast. The horses were housed on the main deck in a wooden shelter towards the rear of the ship.

The four passengers were led below decks by the first mate who introduced himself as "Walter, but everybody calls me Walrus" which was undoubtedly due to his big mustache. They were assigned some very small spaces and had the dining and bathroom procedures explained to them. After a hurried hour of loading extra grain, hay, and water for the horses, they were ready to cast off while the tide was still high.

Adventure awaits, Greylin thought to herself. The huge ropes were lifted off the posts skirting the pier, and one of the sailors blew a deep horn sound on a spiky shell as they turned toward open water.

Chapter 4

THE WINDRACER

"The sea is as alive as any living thing and has as many moods."

- THE BEGINNING OF WISDOM
ATTRIBUTED TO ST. RAUNA

The *Windracer* proved to be a fast ship. The crew of six unfurled her glittering gold and violet sails that were painted with a cloud and sun design, and the land slipped far behind. Greylin marveled at the endless expanse of water that surrounded her in all directions. It made her a bit uneasy, and Finn, who always seemed to sense her mood, distracted her by pointing out seabirds, seals, and fish which seemed to playfully investigate the ship before moving on.

Choppy waves slapped an even tempo at the ship's sides, the temperature dropped as they left the bay, and occasionally, a misty spray would reach them. Ropes groaned and wood creaked as the wind pulled at the sails.

Greylin could not help but look in every direction for solid ground, but there was nothing to be seen. The outer islands soon fell below the horizon behind them. She looked dubiously beneath her at the opaque sea.

The Selkans were right at home above and below the water. Each ship had ladders built on either side—which Finn told her should now be called "port" and "starboard"—and the Selkans thought nothing of leaping off the ship in a graceful dive, swimming rapidly alongside, then climbing back up the ladder onto the ship even when it seemed to Greylin that is was going too fast

23

for them to catch up to it. They always did, though, and she realized it was part of the fun.

Later in the afternoon the wind died down, and there was a perfect silence that seemed to enter into her heart. That night they watched the stars and the slow dance of the moons across the sky. She felt a difference in the Selkans, as though once away from the city and out to sea, they were in their element and free of the judgment of humans. They weren't bothered by her, or the other two humans on board who had been vouched for by Finn, so they behaved with as much joy as they would if they were by themselves. They also whistled a lot and Greylin realized it was a simple language, one that could be heard above the wind and waves.

How, she wondered one day, *does anyone know where they are? It's all the same. How do the fish know where they are? Or where to go and how to get there?* She asked Finn and he explained a lot about the sun and angles and sextants and compasses, currents, and winds, but she didn't completely understand it.

"What does it look like under the water? Does it have hills and valleys? Trees and pathways? she asked Finn.

"Oh, there are hills and valleys, but there is seaweed instead of trees and the pathways the fish follow are made of smells, rhythms and currents."

She silently contemplated that. It didn't seem enough, in her opinion, as a way to find one's direction.

"We use the sun and a compass. I have a small one. I'll get it for you." He ran back to his cot where his pack was and returned with a small round metal case and showed her how it always pointed north. That kept her busy for a while and she went from one place to another testing it out.

Finn's cousin, Capt. Skerry Skellig, was as ebullient as Finn was shy and gentle. He was stocky, friendly, and entertained his passengers every night at the captain's table. He told story after story, some of which sounded like very tall stories to Greylin, but she would never dampen the fun and laughter they were having by accusing him of that. Most tales were about outwitting thieves and ruffians, some were about close calls with storms—those made Greylin very uneasy—and some were about encountering or outrunning the Oarman, which made her uneasy as well, because everyone would give her knowing glances during the tale. But the most disturbing ones were about mysterious disappearances.

"One night..." he would always begin with "one day" or "one night", and then follow with the weather "it was calm and quiet with hardly a wavelet slappin' the bow. Dedira was just a sliver and Enshallah was barely peeping over the horizon, just enough to see a little ways but not be sure of what you saw. I was up in the North Eddan Sea, far to the west because we were avoiding a storm that had gone easterly. We started to make the turn and come about when I see a large, long shape with a hump in the middle. I thought it might be a whale or an island, but distance was hard to figure.

"We turned toward it and sailed on, but we never seemed to get any closer. Dawn came and even with Luma shining down from the sky, I couldn't make out what I was seeing. It seemed sometimes that it was higher than I thought, with a white hump. We sailed a day and a half and got no closer. The men were getting spooked, and since I was accomplishing nothing, I decided to turn back. It wasn't till the next morning that we realized the first mate and the bosun were gone! Completely disappeared and have never been seen since! No one heard a splash, a shout, nor could anyone remember the last time they'd seen them.

"We thought then that what we'd been chasing was the floating island of Edda for which the sea is named. The island has a mind of its own and goes where it will. They say it steals men and keeps them, but sometimes they'd be found floating dead. The two we lost were Selkan, and we hope they still live though where they may be we do not know."

That story left Greylin wide-eyed, but on the way to their cabin, Finn pulled her aside.

"Don't take my cousin's stories too much to heart. A lot of what he says never happened or didn't happen to him. He borrows a lot. He's so entertaining though—and he is the captain—so no one challenges what he says."

Nevertheless, she found it hard to sleep that night. She dreamed she was falling in circles with water whooshing around her. When she awoke, she was dizzy, and realized the ship was pitching from side to side more than usual and going up and then falling down in a stomach-lurching dip followed by a jarring thud as they hit the trough of the wave. The air was chill and damp, and she was feeling sick. She wanted to get up and see what was happening but was afraid she wouldn't be able to keep her balance.

Finn, once again, anticipated her distress and brought her fresh water and a wooden bucket. She was able to sit up with his help, and he showed her how to hold on to the ropes around her cot. She had thought them to be only decorations, but she now realized they had a purpose, and she hung on to them with a death grip. The bucket was for losing supper which she fought against but lost anyway, retching miserably. Finn explained they were heading into a "squall", and it could be rough weather for a while. He didn't seem troubled at all.

The horses were restless as the deck pitched beneath them. She could hear what had to be Bane's heavy hoof upon the deck and Roki would whinny now and again for her. She wanted to go to him but was too nauseated. She had never been so ill. Instead of leveling off, the sea rocked higher. She could hear the men shouting up on the deck. She held on to the ropes and prayed.

Chapter 5

STERREN'S PIQUE

*"The mind may slip away in bits and pieces before
one leaves the body; the last to leave is anger."*

- THE HEALER'S GUIDE TO HEALTH,
1ST EDITION

A blue-coated Mazarine knight galloped along the
East Road toward New Saar. He rode a black Friesian and
pulled one behind. He had been traveling day and night
from Sessirra with news for his order and instructions that
it be immediately forwarded to the king. Once past the
Letto Fens, he crossed the Talla Bridge and took the
northerly Tyhja Ridge Road to avoid the many merchants,
farmers, and visitors crowding through the three great
bridges that linked the southern plains to the island that
held the city of New Saar.

The knight chose instead to cross the great sandy
Heikk Ford north of the island which brought him to a
narrow portcullis which led directly to the Mazarine
stronghold of the Palonen. The gates, in this time of peace,
were open and he loped into the courtyard, scattering a pair
of cats. Four eager pages took the reins of his horses and
led the two exhausted animals away to the stable where
they would be fed, watered, groomed, and healed of their
sore muscles. These were geldings and not likely to snap
at them, unlike the stallions they sometimes had to leave
to the paladins to care for themselves.

The traveler, Sir Mikhael Harras, trotted up the steps
leading to the headquarters of the officer in command. He
passed the first two checkpoints barely pausing to give the
passwords and salute. The warriors guarding the door
knew him by sight and had already judged his urgency.

Within moments he entered the second most formidable chamber in the Palonen: that of the Secretary to the Commander. The first being the Commander himself. The Secretary, a non-combatant—the only one in the building except for those who baked and cleaned—eyed him with keen evaluation.

"What is it, Sir Harras?" he asked without preamble and now barely glancing up as he shuffled his papers.

"An urgent message from Commander Rufter, Mr. Secretary, for the Master Commander regarding an incident in Sessirra which has a direct effect on the possible completion of the First Mission." As Sir Harras announced this he thought he heard a sudden, though muffled, intake of breath from the Secretary. The running joke among the men was that the Secretary was immune to reactions of any kind, so to get a gasp from him was what the men lived for, and Sir Mikhael Harras was no exception. Unfortunately, Harras had no witnesses, nor could he share the news he was delivering with the other men, but it was enough. *He* knew it. *He had done it!*

The First Mission was always the highest priority at the time, changeable depending on needs and conditions. For the last fourteen years, the First Mission had been to locate the missing princess. There had been few reports during the years of searching, and none had held up upon scrutiny.

The Secretary rose, strode to the double doors of the Master Commander's room and opened them announcing: "Sir Mikhael Harras, with urgent news, sir." He then discreetly closed them behind Harras as he entered, knowing full well he would get the story later on.

Sir Harras stopped, saluted, and managed to look the Master Commander squarely in the eye. The man behind the desk rose, returned his salute, and gestured for Harras to sit.

"I prefer to stand, Lord Blackthorne," Harras stated.

"As you wish."

Lord Tarkea Blackthorne, P.E. (for Paladin Emeritus, having married ten years ago) had been the head of the

Mazarine Order for seven years. He was a large, black-haired, copper-skinned man, brother to Kota Blackthorne, who was a Canon of the Vermilion Order, and whose booming voice he shared as a family trait. The Blackthorne family was imposing enough but adding the authority and charisma of Office to them was sometimes dizzying for young recruits.

"This comes directly from Sessirra through Paladin D'Arcannon. He is unable to return because it is imperative that he continue to protect the interests of the First Mission," Harras reported. He then went on to describe the discovery of a child in Maddy Sedge that D'Arcannon believed might be the Princess Cianalas, and the subsequent slaying of the monster called the Oarman by that very child with the aid of a legendary weapon known as the Sword Argente. This meant that the First Arcanum had been attained but also that in the process the Golden Pearl prophecy had been fulfilled.

Harras also reported that Paladin D'Arcannon, accompanied by the Master Mage Heron Hollinghast, was attempting to bring the child back to New Saar by way of the Eddan Sea to Lumenvalo and through the Tyhja mountain pass in order to throw off anyone following them as one attempt at kidnapping had already occurred. They were now at sea.

***

Hours before Sir Harras's arrival at the Palonen, a white arrowswift flew into the aviary atop the Valkoinen Hall and delivered a metal capsule containing a small scroll. The sigil on the scroll marked it as urgent, secret, and indicated which codesong would unlock the writing so it would become visible.

Duren Karhu, a young Lumerian page in dark gray, carefully removed the capsule from the arrowswift's leg. Duren's duties in the aviary were to feed the birds, keep them clean and healthy, and ready them to deliver messages, and receive any that came in. He loved working with the birds, their sleekness, speed, and intelligence never ceased to fascinate him. He had names for all of them. This bird was new to him.

The inscription on the capsule read "sesir>nsar" so he knew it was from the Chapter Hall in Sessirra. He ran down the circular staircase to hand it over to Acolyte Fontannen. Rarely did news come from that part of the world, so he was eager to return and become acquainted with this new bird. How the birds knew where to go was a mystery known only to them and the Master Mages who sent them.

Acolyte Fontannen also noted the origin and destination inscription along with the three sigils, $\Psi\sigma\zeta$, that marked it urgent, secret, and indicated a song he did not know. He hurried down the corridor to Master Ishiki who in turn sent him to find Master Saley, presumably to assist with the singing. He found Master Saley in the garden, singing the roses into blooming early without blemish, and within moments the two masters were behind closed doors singing the message into visibility.

And so it was that the Lumerians reported to King Sterren the news of Greylin's victory over the Oarman and the speculation that she was the Princess Cianalas a few hours before a Mazarine emissary arrived with the same account. To the king's credit, he did not let on to Lord Blackthorne, P.E., that he already knew what the message was that he was about to deliver. And to Blackthorne's credit he did not let on that he knew the Lumerians probably beat him to it.

After expressing his gratitude, Sterren suppressed a surge of fury that this candidate had not already been brought to him. That anger he would reserve for D'Arcannon and Hollinghast when they arrived.

How dare they? He fumed. *They should have brought her to me as soon as they found her. Speed would have protected them more than anything else. Why take her to Sessirra? And put her in danger from that monster! And then they tell me that she killed it? Nonsense, she's just a child. What are they playing at?*

The news that his daughter might be alive and well should have cheered him. While it did for a moment, his anger overwhelmed it, and the heartbreak of the past soon returned to haunt him. He began to brood. Cianalas' mother, Queen Isabela, had been tried and executed for treason because of her love affair with Davin D'Arcannon, Reist D'Arcannon's elder brother. The fact that it was another D'Arcannon who was now withholding his daughter from him made everything that much worse. *What did Isabela call the child? Greyling, or something. First the woman betrays me and then finds a way to steal my child even after her death. Her final insult. And now, when they find her, I am the least of their concerns as they wander about the country. I should have their heads for this!*

Chapter 6

JAARVEN'S STORM

*"My dreams slip through my fingers like
so much sand."*

- LORD WELLSTONE,
HARDAR AND THE OLD ONES

As Sir Mikhael Harras was riding toward New Saar to tell King Sterren the news of his daughter, Archcanon Jaarven Hilde, the king's half-brother, was heading toward the Cathedral. His portly figure was robed in bright red, and as he approached the Cathedral steps, he looked from above like a full-blown poppy being whisked along by the wind through a sea of withered grass. The grass, in this case, being the local tradesmen who parted before him as though they were fainting away from the force of his passage.

When he arrived at his office he had hardly settled behind his desk before a discreet scratching sound from the other side of a hidden door caught his attention. He pulled the maroon curtains aside and opened it to find a shapeless bundle of stinking rags that served as the disguise that obscured his most effective spy, Schretter Mayhap.

"Well?" Jaarven demanded.

Schretter assessed the mood of the Archcanon and stayed lingering in the doorway after bowing nearly to the floor.

"Archcanon, I have news of the girl. There was an attack—"

This Jaarven knew very well because he was the one who had sent members of the Red Hand to find the girl, or any likely girl that could be the princess and bring her back or kill her if that proved impossible. Unbeknownst to him, the men he recruited hired less expensive local thugs in Sessirra to do the work and pocketed the difference.

"—which failed. The details are confusing but during the encounter, the doors blocking the passageway of the monster known as the Oarman were opened. The monster escaped and was killed by this girl who has been recognized as the prophesied 'Golden Pearl' by the people of Sessirra."

Blood drained from Jaarven's face and he wobbled a little from weakness. He staggered over to the chair by his desk and motioned Schretter to come closer.

Schretter shuffled in but kept his distance.

"It is known that she, with a paladin and mage, left on a ship from Sessirra the next morning," Schretter continued. "It is rumored that the ship was headed for Lumenvalo."

Jaarven couldn't seem to grasp the news at first and demanded that Schretter repeat it. He then rewarded him— less generously than if the news had been pleasing—and sent him on his way.

He was furious and sickened. *Why did his plans fail? Why was everyone so incompetent?* He could hardly race around the countryside and do everything himself. He rang for his aide, Father Aulis, and asked for wine, then changed it to brandy. He needed to steady his nerves. He had to plan.

Two glasses of brandy later, he began to see a way to use this as an advantage. They were out to sea. If anything happened at sea, no one could place blame. There weren't many storms at sea this time of year, it was a bit early, but not impossible. All he needed were a few singers. He would tell them that a terrible storm was approaching, he had seen it in a vision sent by ELIEL who showed him it would make landfall and do great damage. Powerful spells were needed to keep it out at sea. They must hold the storm in place and intensify it. Any ship at sea would likely be lost…along with his problems.

He rang again for Father Aulis.

"I need all the Red Hand singers. Have them meet me in the choir area."

"Wouldn't Lumerian Singers be more effective?" Father Aulis asked helpfully.

The Archcanon glared, "I don't want to bother them with something so trivial. The Red Hands will do fine."

"As you wish."

Jaarven leaned back in his chair, closed his eyes and smiled. The Red Hands would ask no questions and do his bidding. He sighed deeply. The whisperwoman was due. That was what he called her, a shadow who tantalized him with her attention. He hoped she would be waiting for him here when he finished instructing the singers.

Chapter 7

LOST AT SEA

"Rain and snow,
And winds that blow,
The roar of waves,
Dark seas below."

-THE SEAFARER'S LAMENT,
ANONYMOUS

The *Windracer* shuddered and groaned as the waves tossed her about. The wind had become a howling roar with no let-up or variation. A steady pounding began that rang through the whole ship. If Greylin had been able to get up, she would have discovered that in the lower level the main mast was surrounded by a huge wooden drum extending all around it like a circular table. It was being pounded on either side by two crewmen with huge mallets, the ends of which were as big as their heads.

They were calling the denizens of the deep for help. If the whales did not save the ship, they would never be able to ride out the storm. The booms made her feel even worse, and she heaved again even though there was nothing left in her stomach, and the heaves racked her body with pain. There was a quick lurch from one side to another, then again, and the ship evened out.

Finn appeared and confirmed that whales had arrived. Even so, the ship still dipped and rose in the waves. Finn didn't seem as reassured as Greylin thought he should be, but she was too sick to even comment. She could barely hear him over the roar of the wind. The ropes were groaning and the boards in the ship were creaking so loudly she thought they would split apart.

"Here," he said, "put your rucksack around your neck, over your shoulder and under your arm, I'll tie it in. Put your sword on, too."

She was little help to him for she was feeling weak as a kitten. He rigged her gear and then told her, "Lean against my back."

She leaned forward and Finn flipped a rope back over both their heads and around their waists and tied her to him.

"We're going up to the horses so hold on."

Finn, who was surprisingly strong for his size, began pulling his way up the ladder to the deck. Then there was another sudden lurch to one side and Greylin remembered nothing afterward.

***

D'Arcannon slid along the top deck carrying as much gear as he could sling on each arm. He made it to the three-sided shelter the horses were in. He saddled Bane and Merelda and was tying down gear onto them when Hollinghast fell onto the deck and slid in at his feet. D'Arcannon pulled him up.

"I CAN'T SING IT DOWN!" Hollinghast shouted, barely louder than the roaring storm. I CAN'T HOLD STILL ENOUGH TO CARRY A TUNE!"

D'Arcannon nodded. "I'M GOING TO TRY TO GET DOWN TO GREYLIN! GET ON MERELDA! WE NEED TO STAY TOGETHER!"

Whether Hollinghast heard him or simply guessed at his intent was unclear. D'Arcannon began the slow process of pulling himself along the deck by safety ropes as the wind pushed at him and screamed in his ears. Before he got halfway along, Finn emerged from below and headed toward him. The wind was at Finn's back, and he slid into D'Arcannon's arms. Together they made it back to the horses. They were all together, but Greylin was hanging limp and pale on Finn's back.

"STAY TOGETHER!" D'Arcannon shouted. Finn nodded.

"GET ON THE HORSES!" Finn shouted. "IF WE GO DOWN THE WHALES WILL—" even as he started to say it, Finn heard the dreaded sound of wood splintering from below decks. There was no time, he jumped on to Roki and hoped the horse would accept him since he was carrying Greylin. The other two mounted and Finn grabbed the reins of both and led them over to the railing.

"IT'S GOING DOWN! WE HAVE TO JUMP!"

He gestured but there was no time to be sure they understood. The ship shuddered and rocked, lifting them so high they would have been flipped right into the sea if it were not for the wall of the shelter. As it rocked back the other way leaning down to touch the dark and angry water, Finn kicked Roki's side and pulled the others. They leaped off the ship and landed in the water, hooves hitting nothing until a vast shape rose slowly underneath them.

"MAKE THE HORSES LAY DOWN. THEIR HOOVES WILL HURT HIS BACK," Finn told them.

To his surprise, Roki laid down as soon as the whale rose to the surface. The other horses did as they were coaxed, and the huge leviathan began to speed them away.

Chapter 8

WASHED UP

*"As much as we think we know of the sea, the wise
ones of the deep know that much more."*

-SESSIRRAN PROVERB

Greylin dreamed she was lying on a beach, at least she
thought it was a beach, because she could hear waves
crashing on the shore and a breeze was cooling her, and
she was not moving. She was thankfully, blissfully still.
She opened her eyes expecting to see the sky but saw
instead the underside of a tent rigged from part of a sail. A
soft snuffle told her Roki was nearby. She reached for him,
and he nuzzled her hand.

She raised her hand to her head, gingerly touching a
large lump. She tried to sit up, but the world spun, and she
collapsed back down again and tried to hold on to the earth
below her as if it was trying to tip her off. When it
subsided, she managed to turn to one side, once more
clutching at the ground as if it was trying to get away from
her. Sand, water, pebbles, and debris were scattered around
her, and a huge cliff covered with vegetation soared
behind. Between her and the cliff were spiky shrubs the
like of which she had never seen before and graceful trees
with long thin leaves bunched on the top. She turned
slowly and painfully to her other side and saw the same
thing with one addition, a cold fire pit and some spits.
That's good, she thought. *That's good. People had to make
that.*

She lost consciousness again and the next time when she awoke, more alert, she grabbed for her sword. In her addled state the first time, it had not occurred to her to check for it before, but now she was coming to her full senses and she panicked. *Thank ELIEL!* The sword was still in the scabbard and that was still firmly tied around her waist. *Was it on me during the storm? Did I put it on? I don't remember. My jewels!* Her hand flew to her waist where the leather belt she made to hide the rings should be. The tiny lumps of the rings assured her they were still there. Daara said the rings were from her mother and told her not to lose them. *And my herbs!* She turned her head to see her rucksack hanging from a branch. *All is well,* she breathed a sigh of relief. She had wrapped them in two oilcloth bags and tied them tightly. She hoped they had stayed dry.

Now, she thought, *I absolutely HAVE TO SIT UP.* She lurched forward. Blood seemed to rush from every part of her body to every other part, but she managed not to pass out again even though the dizziness was sickening. She looked around. There was no one about other than Roki who never left her side. She turned as far as she could in either direction, but it was all the same shoreline. She tried to call out but only a pathetic whisper came out. She focused on the fire pit next to her. Somebody made it. *Where is everyone?*

At that moment, Finn rose up from the ocean's edge right in front of her holding a large *fisal* fish on a sharpened stick. He smiled as she gaped at him.

"You're awake!" he said as he walked up out of the water. "I got us something to eat at least."

"Finn!" she tried to call out but only croaked out something like "Fghh".

He put the fish down and helped her drink from a hollowed-out shell laying near her that she hadn't even noticed.

"All I could find," he said, nodding toward the shell. "We've managed to salvage some things but not the dishes. Drink up. At least we have fresh water.

He pulled the shell away. "Okay, that's enough. Small doses. Little at a time. Take a breath or two and let it settle."

"Where...?" she managed to croak out.

"Well, we haven't found the crew or the captain, or the ship I might add. Hollinghast and D'Arcannon are here, and the horses. They are exploring the island right now. That's how we found the water. We'll move to where the water is now; we were just waiting for you to get better. You whacked your head on the way up the ladder when the ship lurched."

"What happened to the crew?"

"Don't know. Weird, eh? The whales were doing a good job of it, but this was a terrible storm, and it just didn't move on. It set on us and stayed with us. My guess is that the ship broke apart between the stress of the storm and the whales. Their efforts to try to keep it afloat finally crushed it. The whales brought some of us here, and the others, well, somewhere. But remember, they were all Selkans, they could manage better in the water."

He paused. "When things were looking a bit hopeless, I tied us together—do you remember that?"

"No."

"Umm, not surprised. You were so weak. I tied us together, then went up to the horses and got us both on Roki. He let me get on him, too!

Greylin reached over and stroked Roki's nose. "Good boy."

He snuffled.

"It was getting very dark at that point, and I admit I was frightened, but a huge whale carried us along. Then there was ground under our feet, and here we are. Those other two as well, and their horses. Why we're here I don't know, other than the fact that the wise ones knew we needed land and the others could do without. This doesn't improve my liking for boats, though, I can tell you that."

Greylin started to snicker, then broke into a wheezy laugh. Then he laughed, and she laughed harder even though it hurt, and all the stress started to drain away.

"I'll have some more of that water now, thank you," she managed to croak out. "Is there anything to eat?"

He picked up the fish that he caught and twirled it on the stick. "This fish, but I don't think we want to eat it raw. The fire went out and our Lumerian isn't here to relight it with a bit of song. So I guess it's time to catch more fish for all of us and then get some more firewood gathered."

"I can help with the firewood."

He looked at her doubtfully, "Perhaps you should just try to stand up first before you get too ambitious."

Greylin immediately tried to get up and fell back down. She succeeded with a wobbly stance on the second try.

"There! It would probably be a good idea for me to move around," she said.

Roki came over and stood next to her to steady her.

"Look at this! I'll be fine. I can lean on him. You go ahead and find our supper. I'll make my way around."

Finn walked back into the water, dove in, and disappeared under the waves. Greylin took a good long look around. She was glad to be on dry land, but there was very little shoreline. Behind her was the tall cliff she noticed earlier. Cliffs which were surprisingly uniform in size seemed to ring the whole island, though she couldn't see all the way around. She took small steps over to the graceful trees and found some fallen debris that would burn easily. She collected a little at a time as she got used to walking again. She could swear she was still feeling the movement of the ship even though she was on dry land. She made a few trips, dumped the sticks and leaves in the fire pit, and sat back down again to rest and wait.

***

Hollinghast leaned far to the right in his saddle. There was only more ocean and a sheer cliff that continued straight down into the water. He sat back and said, "Just like the other side. No land in sight connecting this."

D'Arcannon nodded, "An island, as we thought."

They turned their horses and headed back to retrace their steps. The roiling storm clouds had finally dispersed and only the occasional gust of wind pulled at them. Yesterday they had explored from their base camp as far to the left as they could travel. The level beach area disappeared into a sheer cliff on that side which matched the one they just observed. They walked their horses and paused after a few miles at a pool formed by a waterfall where they watered the horses.

"I don't know what to make of this turn of events," Hollinghast said as they stared out at the ocean which was now sparkling in the sunlight.

"We are alive. The horses are alive. We are together. Things could be far worse," D'Arcannon replied.

"Indeed! We both felt the evil intent in that storm. You felt the evil; I felt the intent. Neither of us could do anything about it, but to come through as well as we did reveals a grace to be thankful for."

"As long as she recovers," D'Arcannon said quietly and frowned.

"Surely, she will, though the way is not clear to me. What are we supposed to do trapped on this island?"

Chapter 9

EDDA

*"Of the many mysteries of the sea, none is more
debated than the disappearing island of Edda.
There are many who swear they have seen it,
but none that can prove it."*

-ANNALS OF THE SEAFARERS OF SESSIRRA

A few hours later, Greylin was overjoyed to see
Hollinghast and D'Arcannon ride into camp. She rose to
her feet as Hollinghast dismounted and clasped her
shoulders in greeting, then checked the bump on her head.
D'Arcannon beamed like the morning sun. He, too,
dismounted and surprised her by sitting down next to her
when they settled down again.

"You know," D'Arcannon said, "it might be a good
idea the next time to bring along a healer."

"Next time!" Hollinghast exclaimed. "If ELIEL is
good to me, there will never be a next time."

They all chuckled.

D'Arcannon said, "We found water coming down
from an impressive waterfall over that way. We'll move
camp tomorrow and set up there now that you seem to be
doing so well. Finn is doing a great job of feeding us,
nothing much washed up from the ship. I can only hope
that the rest of the crew survived."

"What we're looking for, I think," Hollinghast
interjected, sitting down on the opposite side of the fire pit
and lighting it with a word, "is a way in toward the center.

There are birds flying in and out above the cliffs, so it seems habitable, but we haven't seen a way in, though there are many caves that we haven't explored. We can make out one high mountain in the center that seems to be snow covered."

Finn chose that moment to emerge with a speckled fish he called a "Grouper" which, along with the smaller *fisal* fish, was enough to provide them with a decent feast. Hollinghast, thanks to some singing, was able to stretch out the fuel for the evening, and they were soon warm and well fed. The horses had enough grass to graze on to satisfy them and thanks to the fresh water brought from the waterfall, they were all content.

The sound of the breakers on the shore, the calls of shore birds, and the crackling of the fire lulled Greylin into a peaceful, restful state. She had been put to the test in the last few days and as long as the food, water, and fuel held out, she was reluctant to jump back into the struggle. There were many other birds besides the gulls, some squawking on the cliff-sides, but there was one annoying one that seemed to constantly laugh at them: *ha-haa, hahaha.*

Ha-haa, hahaha.

Ha-haa, hahaha.

The two men filled in their parts of the story to Greylin as they dined on fish. D'Arcannon had gathered the horses and gear and tried to keep everything together. It was thanks to him that they had extra clothes, weapons, and some cooking gear. Unfortunately, none of the foodstuffs survived the saltwater. Miraculously, the horses came through without breaking any legs though they suffered a few scratches when the ship broke apart; however, those had already been treated and healed. The humans and horses had been swiftly picked up by a whale and carried away from the ship's broken and jagged timber, which is probably what kept them from being badly hurt. The transport through the waves in the dark while the wind howled around them was something they would never forget. Finn had concentrated on keeping Greylin's head up and keeping them both close to Roki. Hollinghast had tried to sing the storm down and calm the winds, but he was so buffeted and thrown around that he couldn't manage it.

"Your kantelyre!" Greylin said, sitting up straight in alarm, "Did it get warped by the water?"

Hollinghast shook his head no and lifted the instrument from his chest. "This is a truly magical one. It is not made of wood but from the jawbone of a Sea Pike. Saltwater will not damage it."

Finn looked up, "A Sea Pike? Did you make it? Those are rare and hard to find."

"No, and this is not a very exciting story," Hollinghast said wryly. "I found it in the attic of Holling Hall."

"The attic!" the two exclaimed in surprise. D'Arcannon already knew the story and remained quiet.

"I asked my father where it came from," Hollinghast continued. "He didn't know, so I asked my grandfather. He said that his grandfather had found it in a cave in a high mountain the name of which he never knew. He didn't know how it got there or why, but he said I could have it. I cleaned it, restrung the strings with horsehair and found that it made the sweetest sounds I have ever heard from a kantelyre."

The horses grazed quietly behind them, listening to the tale. They, too, seemed settled and recovered as well. All in all, except for worries about the ship and its crew, they had been extremely lucky. Hollinghast and D'Arcannon split watch and forbid Greylin or Finn to do anything but get a good night's sleep.

The next day they packed up what little they had and made their way to the waterfall. D'Arcannon had understated its beauty. It spilled out of a tall cleft in a green-covered hill and fell in a veil of purest white to a clear pool below. There were mossy banks to rest on and lots of grass for the horses who ate their way around the edges.

After a couple days they noticed an oddity: the position of the sun changed from day to day—where it came up or went down. Once it was setting right in front of them and made a beautiful sparkling path straight out to sea.

"They call that the Glim," Finn said pensively.

"What?" Greylin asked.

"That shining path the sun or the moons make on the water. Selkans find it almost irresistible. They want to follow it out to sea, but if they stay in the sea too long, it is said that they start to change and will eventually turn into *saimaa*.

What's that?"

"Selkans who become seals. They forget their human troubles. That's why we never kill or hurt a seal."

"Why would they want to become seals?"

"If a person is lost at sea, hopeless, or grief stricken, they may choose to 'take the Glim Way' and stay out to sea."

"Do you know anyone who did that?"

"Not personally. But anyone who doesn't return, we surmise that they took the Glim Way. Sometimes you'll see an odd-looking seal basking on the rocks. It's someone in the change."

"But how does a Selkan get lost at sea? Can't they just swim back?"

"Sometimes it's too far out. By the time they get back the change has already happened. We have songs and stories about it. The *Saimaa Pari* for example, the Seal Lovers. A young man fell in love with a beautiful maiden. He went off to sea to make his fortune and his ship was lost in a storm. When he didn't return, she swam out to look for him. He swam back to find her. The story goes that when they found each other they had become seals and never returned."

Greylin gazed thoughtfully out at the ocean. "How would they find each other out there?" she demanded, gesturing dismissively at the wide sea.

Finn started laughing, "Aye, leave it to you to find the flaw in that story."

She laughed. "I mean it!" she managed to say through her giggling as she mock-punched him in the arm. "It's a big ocean. They could easily miss." This set him into another fit of laughing.

'Well," she continued, *"we'd* never know which way to go, the sun keeps changing position. Isn't that how you tell where you are?"

"Aye, and the fact that it keeps changing tells me where we are."

Hollinghast and D'Arcannon perked up at that statement.

"Where?" Hollinghast asked. "Please confirm what I already am guessing."

Finn smiled at him. "The floating island of Edda. The sun isn't moving, of course, we are. We are drifting and turning as we go. This is the island that appears and disappears. I have no idea where in the ocean we are right now."

"How can an island float?" Greylin asked.

D'Arcannon chimed in. "Wouldn't it sink? This land, the rocks, the mountain, how can it float?"

Finn replied, "I've looked underneath while I was out fishing. It's too dark to see down there, and there is a lot of seaweed hanging off the bottom, and I couldn't find anything solid. I could see some kind of tether, as though it's dragging an anchor that really isn't anchored anymore. The island seems to be floating. The only thing I can think of is that there's a big pocket of air underneath us."

They all quieted and considered this. It was disturbing. Greylin for one hoped the island wouldn't spring a leak now that they were on it and decide to finally sink! As they mulled over the information, an eerie cry broke their reverie and shattered the stillness. It came from the interior and didn't sound human, at least not like any sane human, and it didn't come from any animal they had heard before.

Chapter 10

THE HAUNTED CAVERNS

*"The bogies they do tap twice,
the ghosts they make no sound,
the worst of all is the cry
of the banshee wailing all around."*

- GHOST RHYMES OF LANGWER

The eerie cry echoed across the island once more. They froze, listening, and looked at each other. That cry was answered by another and another. Some sounded almost human, some didn't. They seemed to come from all directions except the ocean, but echoes distorted their location. There were few other sounds except for the annoying bird which seemed to mock them: HA-haa, hahahaa.

HA-haa, hahaHAA!

D'Arcannon stood and drew his sword. Hollinghast readied a spell. Finn was still carrying the short sword that Greylin had lent him that was originally D'Arcannon's. The paladin approved the lending. Finn and Greylin both drew their swords.

They could see nothing. Greylin hoped it wasn't another Oarman. She tried to remember exactly what it sounded like so she could compare it to what she was hearing. She thought it was different, but...

D'Arcannon was standing still and listening. Greylin realized he was performing the *nähdä pahaa* or "descrying of evil". Hollinghast's eyes were trying to pierce the dusk for it was growing dark.

As quickly as the noises started, they ceased.

Hollinghast looked at D'Arcannon. "Anything?"

D'Arcannon shook his head. "Not exactly. As evil as it sounded, there seems to be no intentional evil about it, but there is a darkness there that comes with confusion." He frowned, and his forehead knitted in puzzlement. "I think we should have two on guard for the night. Just because something isn't evil doesn't mean it won't attack us."

"Agreed," Hollinghast replied. He looked at Finn and Greylin. "Which one of you two wants first watch?"

"I'll take it," Greylin said. "I don't think I'll be getting much sleep after that anyway."

"Are you sure you're up to it?" he asked.

"Yes," she smiled. "Your healing was effective as always."

"Maybe you missed your calling, Heron," D'Arcannon said as he sheathed his sword. "Maybe you should have been wearing the green robes. Then there wouldn't be all this running about. You could have a nice, comfortable room at a healing center."

"And then who would take care of you?" Hollinghast replied.

"A paladin can heal himself in a pinch," D'Arcannon answered.

"Oh yes," Hollinghast teased. "I've seen that. Scars here and there. I think you all like it that way. You wouldn't like it much if it were your nose that needed reattaching."

"I have never lost my nose!" D'Arcannon sounded affronted.

This, for some reason, sent Greylin and Finn into a fit of nervous laughter. D'Arcannon pushed up his nose and made a face at them which made them laugh even harder and relieved some of the tension.

The night passed without incident or further noises. They decided that a more thorough search of the island was called for, but that they would have to do it together as a group. Getting separated in a place so peculiar and unknown could be disastrous.

They entered the nearest cave in the morning. The cliff sides were riddled with them, but there was so much vegetation and the entrances were so well hidden behind folds in the cliff face, that it was hard to tell which indentations continued on as caves.

As they stepped in, the contrast from the bright sun outside and the gloom within left them blind for a few moments. Hollinghast raised his staff, lighting the end of it with a word that lit up the cavern well enough to proceed. They inched along until D'Arcannon cautioned, "Stop a minute. These caves could go on for miles, twisting and turning, leading to dead ends and branching in many directions. I have heard tales of people entering caves like these and never returning, and people who have managed to return say they were lost for days, sometimes weeks. We need to mark our progress so that we can find our way back."

"Absolutely right!" Hollinghast exclaimed with his usual exuberance, "Now I know why I keep you around, Reist."

"Hah! You'd be lost without me," D'Arcannon replied dryly.

"In this case, literally. Now how shall we do this?"

No one had any chalk, or a long string. The suggestions got sillier for a while, from breadcrumbs to a bag of sand with a hole in it (there were no bags, or bread—though there was lots of sand). Finally, Hollinghast decided that he must resort to magic once more and began composing a spell that would cause a stick to leave a glowing mark along the walls.

Finn suggested that they also add arrow indicators, so that they would know what direction they had traveled in when they made the marks. Developing the spell and the hour of *chantsinging* to accomplish it was going to take some time, so they decided to camp out by the waterfall one more night. As they were sitting around the fire eating their latest fish fry, they heard the eerie cry again followed by immediate answers. All four got to their feet on full alert but could see no one. The horses too, now cued by the behavior of their riders raised their heads and flicked their ears in different directions.

"It's coming from the caves," D'Arcannon surmised.

"Yes, I'm thinking the same thing," Hollinghast answered.

"We'd best be on our guard if we go in them then."

"And why are we going in them again?" Greylin asked.

Hollinghast chuckled. "We need to get off this island. If there is wood or anything where the birds come and go within there, we need to get it."

"Oh," she sighed.

"And eventually we'll run out of wood for the fire. There's not much on the shore here," he continued.

"Well, alright then," she replied.

As the night progressed, they had no more incidents. The next morning Hollinghast began to *chantsing* a set of sticks to mark their passage and they entered the same cave just before noon. There was some discussion about whether or not to bring the horses. They decided it was safer to leave them on their own where there was an ample supply of grass and water. There was no danger of them wandering off the island, and they could do a fine job of protecting themselves if necessary. Roki didn't like it much, but Greylin managed to convince him that they would be right back. At least, she hoped they would.

Hollinghast took his staff, lighting the end of it with a word. The light only penetrated a few feet ahead, though, and sometimes the caverns opened up so high and wide they could not see the walls or ceiling. Sometimes they were so narrow only one person could squeeze through at a time. The walls were strangely smooth and even as was the level floor. Most surprising, though, was when the ceiling opened to the sky letting light flood down. Plants flourished where the sun and rain poured through. Some of these areas were beautiful, like fairy gardens. One even had a small freshwater pool from a tiny waterfall. Silvery minnows darted through its leafy weeds.

Little by little they started to be aware of shadows, sighs, and the sound of footsteps. Each time they could not be sure if someone was there or if they were imagining it. Were they seeing shadows caused by their own light or hearing echoes of their own steps? If they heard something, they would stop, but then there would be nothing. Given the complexity of the caves—and they did have many openings on either side—any creature who knew the caves well could easily elude them.

They stopped for a while to rest in one of the oases of light where five different tunnels opened before them. The caves seemed to go on and on and they felt like they were making little progress. They made a light meal of leftover fish while they considered how to proceed.

"Finn, can you see ghosts?" Hollinghast asked softly.

"What?" Finn asked, startled.

"We need to separate out what we are seeing. Greylin and I can see them. D'Arcannon cannot. I need to know if you can so that we can determine what we are seeing."

"I didn't think there were such things...or that you could see..." Finn's voice trailed away as he digested this revelation. "So... you can," he continued, more to himself than to Hollinghast. Then he replied, "Few Selkans can. I know I can't. Or haven't. I didn't think they existed."

"Oh, they do," Hollinghast assured him. "So now that we know that, Finn, you and Greylin watch the two tunnels to the left. D'Arcannon and I will watch the three on the right. If you see something, check with the other person and determine if you both saw it, or if only the ghost seer did."

Greylin and Finn agreed on hand signals. Upon a sighting, they would each raise a finger for each shape they saw.

They all waited quietly for a few minutes. Then once again, they thought they heard soft sounds: A sigh, or shuffle, then maybe a footstep or two. A dark shape moved quickly past and Greylin looked at Finn. She raised one finger. Finn did not.

Greylin looked quickly over at Hollinghast, he signaled D'Arcannon who shook his head in negative. *So these things* were *ghosts!*

D'Arcannon looked frustrated because he could not fight what he could not see. Greylin had never seen Finn look scared before, but the thought of being surrounded with ghosts made him look as though someone had poured ice water over him.

Hollinghast prepared a flash shock, one that was known to repel ghosts. It was the same spell he had used the night that slinkhounds burst into the cottage Greylin shared with Daara when he saved her from an attack so long ago. That night had started their journey together. In order to use such a spell in an emergency, it had to be prepared ahead of time, and there would be no time to sing a spell as powerful as a flash shock if they were under sudden attack. He stored his spells with a technique called *loitsusäilö* that would allow him to release them with a single word. The drawback was that over time, it faded. He didn't want to take a chance letting loose a spell that didn't work so he was quickly renewing it.

They waited until he finished. There were no more noises. No cries. No attacks. They decided to move on.

Chapter 11

UKIYO

"Plum blossoms turn to the light
of an ever-changing sun
as we drift in silence,
on the winds of heaven."

- POEMS *BY ASUKE THE YOUNGER*

They could not resist looking anxiously behind them from time to time as they traveled along. Hollinghast was in front with his staff lighting the way. Greylin followed him, then Finn behind her, and D'Arcannon took rear guard. All around them the noises followed: shuffles, footsteps, sliding sounds or sighs. Something, or some things, watched and followed but never came near enough for them to see what they were. Their nerves were frayed from listening and looking for shapes that they could never clearly see. It was hard to know which was worse, the bloodcurdling wails they had heard at the camp or the soft shuffling sounds that their ears strained to hear.

Another pocket of light beamed from around the next corner. These openings to the sky were heartening even though it exposed them brightly to the things which trailed them. They rounded the corner expecting to see another patch of sunlight and ferns. Instead they were stunned to see the tunnel open to a broad vista beneath them.

Spreading out from the foot of the cliff were miles of lush greenery in what appeared to be a circular valley surrounding a cone-shaped mountain the center of which climbed so high it was snow-covered at the top. The valley was luxuriant and fragrant with the scent of flowers that now wafted up to them on a gentle breeze. Gulls cried above and songbirds trilled from below. Every square foot was covered with vegetation, including patches of fields and terraced hillsides. As they looked more closely, they realized they were viewing a city of houses whose rooftops formed a continuous garden. Vines climbed up trellised walls and hung down from leafy rooftops. Pathways to and from each house were lined with plants and bushes as was every place in between. They could see tiny figures in the distance walking here and there along the lanes.

They had found a way in! Now all they had to do was find a way down. The cave's opening where they stood was at least eighty hands up the cliffside. They examined the wall below... there were few handholds, but it was enough of a fall to cause injury, and they had no rope.

While they were trying to think of solutions, someone noticed them from below.

"Ho! Gake no eu de!"

"Helloo!" D'Arcannon replied. He had the loudest voice.

"Moshi!... ahh, I think — hello!"

"Can you help us get down?"

"Wait there!" the man answered. "I'll get help."

Whoever or whatever was in the caverns, they were surely not the people who lived below.

Why, Greylin wondered, *are there no tales of these people? Is it because no one escapes once they arrive?* She looked out over the valley that was kissed with mist here and there, only broken by shards of sunlight that touched the tops of mulberry and fruit trees. *Maybe they don't want to.*

Eventually a climbing team of two with hammers and spikes, equipped with a rope ladder made their way up to the rock shelf and the group began their descent. Hollinghast had taken the time to carefully mark the entrance to the cave in case they needed to make an exit. He noted that the spikes remained in the cliff. That would be helpful.

A group of people dressed in linen tunics that were cinched with brightly woven silk sashes gathered below them. They seemed excited but were smiling. D'Arcannon hoped the smiles were welcoming and not anticipatory of having them for dinner because it would be quite a battle. They were a fine-boned people and he could easily take a few of them down, but they also looked wiry and fast, so protecting the whole group would require speed. Oblivious of these concerns, the inhabitants ushered them through a maze of lush green leaves; some vines climbed up stalks of strong plants like corn, some hung from rooftops that were planted with flax or wheat. There were vegetables, fruit, and flowers everywhere.

D'Arcannon decided to turn on the charm and explained that he and his friends were victims of a shipwreck in a terrible storm. The islanders identified themselves as the s*hinwazoku* and expressed much sympathy. They explained that this had happened before which is why they could speak his language.

"There are others like us?" he asked.

"All dead now," was the answer which only served to make him more wary.

The group led the castaways to a large pavilion which was supported by tied cornstalks and roofed with wide leaves. It was open on all sides which allowed everyone to see the new-found travelers. As they entered, a couple introduced themselves as Sato and Koren. Sato, the woman, was tiny and wizened with happy wrinkles around her blue eyes. Her hair was still mostly dark, but a streak of white on each side gave her the look of wearing wings of wisdom. Koren was older, stockier and had an air of authority.

The newcomers were brought an assortment of luscious fruits from the surrounding gardens which the *shinwazoku* placed shyly before them. Hollinghast surreptitiously checked them for poison and gave them the all clear. There was also a stew of vegetables and noodles and shreds of something unidentifiable. As they ate, some of the fruit was passed around and all participated.

It was Sato and Koren's son, Samon, who had been the first one to see the group on the cliff, and this seemed to give the family a certain right of ownership of the group's exotic—to them—presence. Their daughter Rilah watched them shyly as she sat next to her mother. She seemed to be about only a little older than Greylin and Finn. The newcomers were a sensation, but it was Finn they were the most interested in. They had never seen a Selkan before but had heard about them from Sato's blue-eyed grandfather, a former castaway. A few of them began composing a song about Finn and the singing and laughter filled the background of the evening.

As they related their journey through the caverns, Koren nodded, and explained that the cries were from what he called the *kūfuku no yūrei,* the "hungry ghosts".

"After we came to this place many generations ago," he gestured with his hand making an arc above him, "they would appear from time to time perhaps from a shipwreck. One who did not die and lived here for a long time—and he is the first one who taught us your language—he said there was a wreck in a storm, much like yours, and the survivors tried to swim to the island, but the wood from the wreck must have caused our ship, what you call an island, to move away. It is still able to do that and keeps us safe. It moves out of the path of large things like rocks or ships which is why we have not foundered on rocks before this.

"He said that the others drowned on the way, but he was able to make it. Their strong desire and fear seemed to continue in shadowy versions of themselves swimming next to him and walking up on the shore. We believe those are the ghosts in the caverns. They made it here, they remember their desires and their hunger, but they shun the light and cannot eat or be comforted. Perhaps it was the smell of your cooking that caused them to cry out.

"He had the blue eyes. He is our great great grandfather," Koren continued. He nodded at Sato. "Many different marriages since but our daughter Rilah has the blue eyes. Very rare."

Rilah smiled shyly. Her dark hair and blue eyes were striking.

"But shouldn't their souls have returned to ELIEL?" Greylin asked.

"I do not know of this ELIEL," Koren continued, "but there is a deep soul which returns to the creator to be sent forth again, but for those who die so violently and in fear, those intense energies can persist, broken off on their own."

Greylin was so stunned at Koren's admission of ignorance of ELIEL that she had nothing to say. *I assume so much,* she thought, *and only wind up showing my own ignorance of the world.*

Polite but reserved, Hollinghast did not bring up the question of how they might be able to leave. He let that rest for the moment, but his mind ticked off book after book, scroll after scroll, trying to remember anything he might have read that pertained to the *shinwazoku* and the island. Nevertheless, the food, firelight, and the gentle, lilting songs they sang before retiring for the night were comforting. They would still keep watch, but there was no evil here.

"I just noticed something," Greylin said after dinner, lifting her head. "That bird, the ha-ha one. I don't hear it anymore."

"Oh yes, the HAH-ha, ha-ha-haa bird," Koren said, imitating the bird perfectly.

"Yes, that one," she answered.

He looked at their empty bowls and nodded. "Very good eating," he said rubbing his stomach.

All four looked down at their bowls in stunned silence, all except for D'Arcannon whose soft chuckle broke the stillness.

***

The next day in the brightness of the morning light as they breakfasted on sweet fruit and grains, they brought up the subject of leaving the island.

"We are grateful to you for rescuing us, and grateful also for your hospitality. There are pressing matters that call us to home, however, and we must inquire of you how we can accomplish that," Hollinghast stated.

That was very diplomatic, Greylin thought, *I wonder how far that will get us?*

Koren frowned thoughtfully and looked at his wife. She looked at Hollinghast kindly and said, "I do not know how that can be done. We cannot spare the few fruit trees we have for the building of a vessel. And there is no easy way to bring it from here to the shoreline even if you were to construct something."

"Is this why no one has heard of the *shinwazoko*? How did you first come here?" D'Arcannon asked.

"Same as you," Sato answered. "We were stranded. Except we did not come from the sea. We came from the stars.

Hollinghast reacted with a start but said nothing.

"This," she gestured with her arms the whole of the island, "is our ship. It is called the *Ukiyo*, the floating world. We did not expect to come here. Our dream was to float through the stars forever, gathering light on huge solar sails. We have everything we need. Why should we desire else? Our ship was designed to avoid objects, but a meteor came so quickly we could not avoid it, and we were lucky to fall into the ocean of this place."

Koren explained, "That was hundreds of years ago. The dome above was broken away and our corridors became caves. Our great wing," he pointed to the top of the center mountain, "is above us. The other is below us, broken," he said. He pointed down. "We will always float. The *Ukiyo* can make fresh water from the sea, separates the salt out for our use, and fills the under corridors with air. As long as the sun shines, we are safe." He smiled.

"And you never tried to leave?" Finn asked.

"Why? We cannot return to our home. It is peaceful here, and safe. That is what we wanted. It is as good as any other place if not better. Our ancestors were running away from a terrible war. Why would we want to leave?"

"My brother did," Rilah piped up.

"Rilah! You don't know that," Sato chastised.

"Did he?" D'Arcannon smiled, catching Rilah's eye. She darted a look at her mother. Choosing rebellion, she answered. "My brother wanted to see the rest of the world. It was years ago. He climbed to the top of the snow mountain and wore the Elder Crown that was placed there hundreds of years ago by the *Akarui Josei*."

She turned and pointed to the high mountain in the center of the island that her father had just indicated. "It is in a cave at the top. He had to leave it for the *Akarui Josei* to find on her return, but he only wanted to use it, just once. He said it showed him that there would be a ship, and he needed to watch for it. He had only to wait for one, he said, and then light a signal fire. He would have to swim or float on a raft because the *Ukiyo* moves away from ships. One day we saw the smoke on the shoreline. We went to look for him, but he was gone."

"We never heard from him again," Sato said, sadness drawing down the corners of her mouth.

The *shinwazoko* were a beautiful people. Their fine features and high cheekbones reminded Greylin of someone, someone so handsome that it all came together as she looked at Rilah's blue eyes and realized who she resembled.

"Rilah," Greylin asked. "What is your brother's name?"

"Rilann," she answered.

Both Hollinghast and D'Arcannon were following Greylin's thoughts and conclusions. Rilann Blake was the most handsome man Greylin had ever seen, one who she had encountered at the Kilgari camp in the desert on their way to Sessirra. He had seen right through her disguise as a boy and handed her a rose. Hollinghast and D'Arcannon informed her that he was a spy for the King of Castabal, and not someone they trusted. They should have noted the resemblance to Rilah right away.

"I think you are right, Rilah, and I think we know him," Greylin said.

"I knew it!" she exclaimed. "I knew he made it!"

Koren and Sato wanted to know every bit of news about him. Hollinghast and D'Arcannon took over the conversation from there. They told them what they knew of Rilann but whitewashed their opinions. Greylin was intrigued by Rilah's story, but more intrigued by something that had caught her attention even more: The Elder Crown. Once again, her mind raced down corridors of time. Sensations flooded in and past and present imploded in a jumble of unsorted feelings and images.

Chapter 12

THE CROWN OF THE CRESCENT MOON

"One theory put forth is that there are multiple realities imposed upon each other in such a way that any decision one makes propels a soul into a single reality at the expense of the others which then continue on their own. This has been declared heresy by the Council and Synod as being opposed to the Principle of Clarity as written in the Confessions *by Archcanon Paulus Incipe."*

-MEDITATIONS AND CONTEMPLATIONS
BY TIMON THE HERMIT

Greylin's mind kept racing, and she found that once again she was unable to talk. She withdrew to one side of the pavilion to rest and try to tame the tumult raging inside her. The others were caught up in discussion, and no one paid attention to her. She closed her eyes and tried to let her consciousness drift into a more peaceful state, but her mind refused to quiet, and snatches of sentences came and went that were spoken in different voices. Visions of the Elder Crown kept coming at her, and the words *"Crown of the Crescent Moon"* imposed itself upon it.

Greylin knew what the crown looked like without being told. It was an opalescent circlet formed by delicately molded eversilver in the shape of leaves, flowers, and berries with a crescent moon in the center. It was beautiful, exquisitely made. It was calling to her...waiting for her. *How could I have forgotten it?* she wondered. She yearned for it the same way she had hungered for the Sword Argente that now hung at her side.

It was happening again, only this time it was a crown. A crown she wanted more than life itself. She shivered on her sleeping mat and tried to keep her teeth from chattering. She was hot, then cold—shivering then sweating—sick with longing. *Maybe I am simply ill, and this yearning is a deranged symptom.* Even as she thought this, she was listening to hear if everyone was asleep.

They had posted double watches in an overabundance of caution. Finn would be on second watch with Greylin. She made a show of retiring, but when everyone else was asleep, quietly slipped away. They wouldn't be concerned until they changed watch. At a fast run she could make it to the mountain before they noticed she was missing.

The second moon, Enshallah, was high and full so she had no difficulty seeing the mountain in the moonlight and making her way to it. The vegetation that seemed maze-like at first glance radiated in paths from the center of the island. She ran lightly toward the tall mountain and within an hour was at the base. She stopped and looked up. In the moonlight she could see a dark spot near the top. *That must be the cave,* she thought. *It is an ice cave and the climb is going to be treacherous.* She wasn't sure where to begin and walked back and forth at the base looking for a way up.

It all looked the same, lumps and bumps with no clear path. She took out her sword on a hunch and waved the tip back and forth. Was that a quiver in one direction? Again, the sword seemed to tell her *"Here!"* and she obeyed. She sheathed her sword and began to climb, using the lumps and bumps to pull her way up.

She thanked ELIEL for the light of the second moon which helped her see each handhold. The ice mountain was nearly straight up, and she had to look carefully for every indentation. Even so, it was easy going compared to what she encountered when she hit the snow line. It was cold and slippery, but easier to see the surface in the reflected light of the moon. Everything that was below or behind her was in comparative darkness, and with nothing to see, she suffered an illusion of crawling along a floor pulling a large weight instead of going straight up the side of a mountain. It was a kind of delirium that wouldn't stop, and she knew that being lulled by it could cause her to make a mistake and plunge to her death. Added to that was the cold that was crippling her hands. She could not be sure if she was holding on to an outcropping because her fingers were completely numb. *If I come out of this with any fingers left after the frostbite eats them it will be a miracle,* she thought. Then she realized she still had a knife in her ankle sheath. She took that out and chipped at the ice until it held. Then she pulled the sword. Holding it downward she tested it on the ice. It slid in and held and if the ice was no more than soft wood. *There is so much more to this sword than I could have guessed,* she thought.

Even with that help, it seemed like hours before she crawled in and collapsed at the entrance to the cave just as the sun was coming up and Enshallah set. Her arms were shaking from the strain, but the daylight helped her feel grounded and less dreamy. The cave was over a hundred hands long and dead straight. She could see the crown, sitting atop a platform, but directly behind it was an ice dragon eying her with hatred.

Daara, the woman who had taken her away to safety as a child and then never brought her back, had told her there were no such things as dragons, but then, Daara didn't believe in ghosts either. Daara also thought that a woman casting a spell would bring a plague among the people. Daara also said she knew how to read yet when she opened the one *Book of the Covenant* they owned, she tried to recite it by memory. Greylin grimaced, it seemed everything Daara had ever told her was questionable!

The crown glimmered with a pearly glow, and as the first rays of the sun touched it, rainbows leaped from faceted crystals and danced across the wall. The ice dragon was just as beautiful. His scales were like prisms of ice reflecting every bit of light; his eyes were as blue as a summer sky. Greylin sat and took in the beauty. He did not approach her, and she didn't move.

The dragon wasn't much bigger than she was. The myths—*well, guess they weren't myths after all*—said ice dragons were known to be small, this one was no exception.

"Hello," she said, testing out his reaction. He spit out some frost. *How am I supposed to get the crown from him?* She wondered. *How did Rilann do it?* She didn't want to do battle with the creature. Her instincts said not to fight for the crown, and that the dragon was an important part of what she had to do…but what was it? She thought she could probably win against him if she had to. He was smaller than the Oarman, but he was so dazzling. *Beguiled by beauty,* she thought wryly, *a fitting way for a possible-princess to die.*

Greylin leaned back against the wall. *At least he isn't attacking, just glaring.* She looked around at the ice-covered walls and sighed. *What am I doing here?* She had an attack of homesickness and loneliness. She had so few friends, why had she left her new ones behind? She trusted Hollinghast and D'Arcannon more and more even though she knew their loyalties were to their Orders and King Sterren first. She trusted Finn, and Roki who waited for her out on the beach. She hadn't seen Roki since they left to search the caves. She hoped he was alright. With that thought she immediately got a vision of green grass, warm sun, and fresh water from the waterfall. The waves were caressing the shore, and birds were calling and flying over the cliffs to the gardens within the valley. She thought about how much she missed him and made a mental snapshot of the predicament she was in.

To her surprise she got an immediate acknowledgment in the form of a return vision, a little distorted, of what she had just sent, but she knew it was from him. She sat bolt upright. They were communicating! They always had, but more in the usual horse and human way. This was different, more immediate and solid. Then something very strange happened: She got a mental image of herself sitting at the mouth of the cave. Who could see that? Only the dragon.

If she could communicate with Roki, and he could communicate with the dragon, then she should be able to communicate with the dragon through him. She sent a mental image of the fondness she felt for Roki. The grooming, riding, feeding, sleeping next to him, all those things from their daily lives that showed kindness and trust. And then she waited.

The dragon groaned in a slightly disgusted way. She couldn't help laughing. He wasn't glaring anymore, so she got up slowly and moved toward him. He didn't spit frost. She sent a picture to Roki of her picking up the crown and waited for him to relay it to the dragon. He spit a little more frost then. Not a lot, but she knew he didn't like it. She tried then, to ask what he wanted, why he was guarding it, and for whom. She got a picture of a well-dressed woman and realized that part of her problem was that she looked rough from a shipwreck and was dressed in Selkan sailor clothes. *Drat! I didn't think that would be in the way.* Had Roki ever seen her dressed up?

Yes, he had seen her after she killed the Oarman! Hollinghast had taken the farm boy obfuscation spell off and then thrown a glamour on her in place of it which transformed her into the "Golden Pearl", the prophesied lady of the Sessirran legend. Roki had broken out of his stable and come to her, sensing the danger she was in. She showed him that scene from her point of view. He showed her the scene from his. She was startled to see her own transformation.

Greylin hadn't encountered a lot of mirrors in her life. There were none on the farm—she and Daara couldn't afford something so fine—and since then there had been a lot of running around the countryside and camping out. She had only seen herself a few times. She realized now that even when she did, she always had the farm boy look except for a couple instances after a healing where she saw her true self. Now, looking through Roki's eyes as he saw her on the night she killed the Oarman, she beheld a shimmering vision of a beauty. *Was that me? Is that how I looked?* She was fascinated by it, she had to admit, and had a hard time moving past it, but the Elder Crown called her.

She looked at the dragon, and he looked at her. He wasn't going to attack, and she thought he understood that she wasn't going to hurt him either. She pictured what she looked like at that moment of victory in Sessirra and willed that image to the dragon. Nothing happened. She thought of that image and the dragon she was seeing at the same time and sent it to Roki though she wondered how in Rauna's name he was supposed to sort out what she wanted.

Whatever he thought, or sent, the ice dragon's demeanor changed completely. He started purring! Or something that sounded like a purr. He put his head down, his nose out, and purred at her. She moved closer to the crown. *Still purring.* She mentally thanked Roki for all he had done, whatever it was, and moved forward carefully. The dragon stretched out to her, still purring, and she tentatively touched his nose. He purred louder.

Good, she thought, *this is working.* She gently rubbed his nose while her other hand reached for the crown. He scared her once by moving closer and rubbing up against her. She stroked his long neck and marveled at the sheen and rainbow patterns in his scales. Now he was practically knocking her over with affection. She picked up the crown and backed up a little. If she could keep the dragon off her… *Who has problems like this? Only me,* she thought as she slipped the crown on her head.

It was like getting struck by the weight of a heavy wave. It knocked her flat on her back, paralyzed by the forces running through her. If she thought about anything—her next move, something as small as sitting up—door after door of possibility opened up. Every little idea that started to form created a path and that path went to many possible directions. One door after another would slam open revealing doors ahead and to either side. As she thought to move forward, the doors would click-click-click-click open to possibilities. It was too much. Endless.

Too overwhelming. She tried to focus on one thing: getting the crown off her head.

She must have succeeded, or maybe the dragon knocked it off, mercifully, because he was licking her face. An ice dragon isn't particularly drooly or sticky, so having her head licked by his cold tongue was oddly pleasant. She just lay there for a few moments before sitting up.

Chapter 13

VISIONS

"Knowing the future could be as much a curse as a blessing. What is preordained, what is changeable?"

- THE LETTERS OF QUEEN HIILDA OF SAAR

I should have a plan, Greylin thought. *This crown is not just a pretty thing. It called to me, and I obsessed over it the same way I did with the sword. There is purpose here, destiny, and very good reasons why this is all happening. Think!*

Her mind struggled to focus but kept being overrun by the intensity of the visions she had just experienced. When she wore the crown, she saw paths, doorways, and possibilities. All of that occurred if she thought of the future, even though it was only a moment ahead in the future, something as simple as sitting up.

What about the past? Let's try the history of the Sword Argente. Will it tell me the mystery of it? She took a deep breath, focused her eyes on the sword, and put the crown on again.

This time a path seemed to appear behind her. She saw it with her mind, not her eyes, and it was disconcerting to "see backwards". A shining path led back to Sessirra, the death of the Oarman, Greylin's first sighting of the elaborate scrollwork on the doors barring the passageway to North Bay, and then there was a brief flash of her growing up, a whole lifetime in a few moments.

She saw herself in Maddy Sedge, working the farm, looking like a boy, then younger hiding from her stepfather, riding in an open wagon as a baby, the shocking verification of all that she questioned. She saw herself being smuggled out of Castle Hilde, her mother pacing in her room, white with terror, as she waited for guards to take her away.

She saw herself as a baby dressed in a beautiful satin and lace gown as she was baptized the Princess Cianalas Hiraeth di Castabal Hilde. Until that moment she had thought it was not true. She thought the "real truth" would come out and she would be sent back to Maddy Sedge and not have to take on the crushing responsibilities that were hovering in wait for her. Instead the truth turned out to be the opposite of what she expected.

A quiet stillness grew as the sword waited. Time passed, and many things sped by like shadows that were not part of the story, then there was an older woman, carrying the sword up the cavern steps in Sessirra, and she realized with a start that she was looking at herself in a former life. The woman knew she did not have much longer to live and that she had to leave the sword for herself somewhere safe, somewhere it wouldn't get stolen, where no one would recognize it for what it was.

The story turned backward again and she saw the sword being made, the ore taken from mines of eversilver by a man with white hair and blue eyes. Spells were worked upon it beyond the hills of Langwer by the dark shapes of smiths hammering against the red firelight of their forges. Even then the sword was not finished, and it was taken further into the hills where—

St. Rauna! She still lived!

Greylin watched as Rauna placed her hands upon the sword and prayed that ELIEL imbue it with intelligence and loyalty. She looked up at Greylin then, from across centuries, looked right into her as though she was standing there—now—as herself, as if she could see Greylin, sitting on the floor of the ice cavern next to a dragon. Rauna was love personified. She poured forth strength, hope, courage, and wisdom, filling Greylin to completion.

"Rauna," Greylin whispered with intense longing and reached out to her, but even as she did, Rauna seemed to shrink and pull away into the distance. Greylin dragged the crown off her head and sobbed a forgotten grief overwhelmed her.

The dragon started licking her frantically and squeaking which struck her as so ridiculous her crying finally turned to giddy laughter. He padded to the entrance to the cave and shook out his wings, making them rattle fiercely. Then he turned and looked at her.

It was an obvious invitation. She walked over to him. "Can you carry me?" she asked. She sent Roki a picture of her on his back. She got a picture back of that, only with her lying flat along the dragon's back, gliding gently downward. She realized that he could carry her down but was not strong enough to carry her up. She shoved the crown in the back of her shirt and lay down along the dragon's back.

He was only a few hands longer than she was, not counting his tail which was almost as long as his body. He jumped off the edge and his wings stretched out. They were much bigger and longer than she thought once he had room for a full wingspread. Each wing was three times his length. They glided slowly and gently down. He let her off, nudged her affectionately, and with only one backward glance took off again flying over the cliffs to the ocean. *Home,* she realized, *he's going home. He's waited so long!*

They must have been seen—*who could miss that?*— and she knew it wouldn't be long until her friends found her. They'd be angry at her again. She sighed and sat against the base of the mountain to think. *I only have a few minutes by myself. I need to know what to do, why I have this crown, and what it is supposed to tell me. I'll try looking to the past again. Maybe that will tell me how to use it.*

There were no houses nearby so she would have a few moments to rest. A light rain started to fall, and the sound of the raindrops seemed like they were too loud, the rain too wet, the sky too bright, the smell of the luxuriant flowers like a cloud in her nose. Wearing the crown must have heightened her senses. She closed her eyes and leaned back. Gingerly she took the crown in her hands. *I have to know.* She opened her eyes and focused on the crown, took a deep breath, and placed it once again on her head.

Another vision formed of a scene behind her head. The crown was sitting in its place in the cavern; the ice dragon guarding it. Then Rilann entered! *How had he managed it?* she wondered. He dragged in a bag…it was full of fish! He emptied it and left the cavern. The dragon inched forward and ate all the fish, gorging himself into a stupor. Then the beast shuffled back, lay down in a circle around the pedestal of the crown, and fell asleep.

Rilann then appeared again over the lip of the cavern. He reached over the body of the sleeping dragon and picked up the crown, then walked to the mouth of the cave and put it on. Greylin was gratified to see him slammed backwards like she had been. *At least I'm not the only one!* He lay there a moment or two then pulled off the crown and replaced it. He must have gotten the information he wanted because he left. *Did he see the arrival of a ship, when it would approach, how to signal it? He must have because obviously it had worked.*

Then there was a long pause where the crown just sat there waiting. She saw an old woman taking the crown— then realized she was placing it, not removing it, and knew she was looking once more at her former self.

The crown was made to hold the gift of seeing; it was imbued with magic under the moons when all three were in the sky. It was crafted with songs in a language she did not understand with music that seemed to weave in and out with different melodies interacting together.

The crown was made at the same forges as the sword and given to this woman—to her. It was meant to be used as a way to choose the right path by seeing the outcome of whatever path was chosen. It was not only called the Elder Crown and the Crown of the Crescent Moon; it was also called the Path of Indecision. While it could show good choices, it could also show the consequences of every bad choice, and some choices had no good outcomes. She pulled off the crown, leaned over, and tried not to heave.

Oh no, please don't let my friends arrive right now. They did, of course, at that very moment.

"Greylin!! Are you alright?"

Voices. *Too loud. Who was who?*

"Yes, fine, just a little dizzy." she managed to squeak out.

"Where did you go? We were looking all over for you!"

"What was that in the sky falling from the mountain?"

"Are you hurt?"

"Why didn't you tell me where you were going?"

She couldn't sort out who was speaking.

"I need a few moments. Just let me rest here. Don't talk for a while."

This had the predictable effect of making them talk even more. She groaned. This prompted them to pick her up and carry her back to their lodging. She opened her eyes and realized that it was D'Arcannon carrying her. Again. She found it most enjoyable and put her arms around his neck and leaned into him a bit. She was wondering if there was a way to get him to take the long way around when she was placed down on her sleeping mat. She sighed with regret, *well, that was over too soon.*

They had already spotted the crown. There was no use trying to hide it, it was too big to hide. D'Arcannon eased her down gently, thinking about the first time he had picked her up from the floor of the little cottage in Maddy Sedge. He had thought her no more than a scrawny ten-year-old boy no taller than his elbow. Then there was the rescue from the camp of the Kingsguard. She had already grown a bit by then once the healers had taken off the old spells that were holding her back. He pondered the change in her, *she's grown to my shoulder already and sure is putting on some weight!*

Chapter 14

THE KING OF CASTABAL

"The king is in his castle, the maid upon the strand.
The queen she is a-riding, and peace becalms the land."

- CASTABAL CHILDREN'S RHYME

Rilann Blake entered the courtyard of the Torilinna castle grounds in Rimmon riding a Kilgarin blood bay horse of perfect conformation. He handed the reins to an attendant liveried in the violet and silver colors of Castabal and headed to his spartan quarters in the rear of the royal wing.

The gardens were in full bloom, blossoming earlier than had been the case in Taivasta and certainly lusher than any oasis in the Kilgarin desert. The combined scents of the flowers and the sound of fountains splashing seemed decadent after spending so long in wilder, more desolate lands. Everything was so—*civilized!*

It took him a while in his quarters to bathe, shave, don clean clothes, and trim his hair and nails before he was ready to report to the king. His news was important but not so urgent that he couldn't be presentable. He didn't want to distract with grubbiness, and the king was noticeably distracted by such things.

Luckily it wasn't Garrenday when the king held court and ruled on appeals from the lower courts. That would take all day and he would have to wait. Today, Aniraday, was a private session day so it was perfect timing.

Rilann presented himself before the privy chamber. Both guards knew him and Captain Verano nodded and immediately slipped through a door to notify the king. He returned in a moment to usher Rilann in with a nod.

The young king, Oro Develen di Xanchez Castillo, beloved of his people, the one they nicknamed the Day Star, stood by a mahogany table large enough to seat twelve but now only accommodated him, two others, and an assortment of maps spread upon it. He crossed to Rilann and placed his hands on Rilann's upper arms in greeting. The king's hair was dark, tied back at the nape of his neck, and he had the same flashing dark eyes that had made his older sister the beauty she was.

"I was worried about you! Though you look in perfect health as usual. What news do you bring?" he asked.

"My Prince," Rilann bowed. The proper address would always be "Prince" even though the man, now in his thirties, was already king.

"It is not good—may I?" he crossed to the maps and acknowledged the other two gentlemen. One was Sergei Illyich, the prince's Captain of the Horseguard, a pale blond with piercing blue eyes. The other was Tauro Sandovar, General of the Army, a short man whose size belayed his strength of character. Exactly the people he wanted to see.

Rilann lost no time in pleasantries, "The Jonji are amassing in great numbers on the other side of the Tammerlin Strait." He tapped the map spread on the table. "I swam across, here, at night to see what they were up to and they captured me."

The king gasped in dismay at this news.

"This is why it took so long for me to return," Rilann continued. "But it allowed me to observe them longer. They are moving west. I do not think it planned, but it is shared, like a migration or expansion due to large numbers. They have no language that I could discern. I think food, territory, or something they need is getting scarce. There was fighting among them and when an enemy was killed, he or she was consumed by the others. Most of them were thin which makes me think a lot of it was due to a problem with their food supply."

"Rilann! They could have just as easily eaten you!" the king exclaimed.

"And I am just as surprised as you that they didn't, Sire," he replied. "I thought I was doomed, but they are creatures of extreme habit. It seemed like they didn't know what to do with me. They only killed when they were on the move—and when they switched from chanting "jonji" to the "shalan". They killed on the "shalan" which is a hushed, whispering kind of chant."

"They really do that then?" the king asked.

"Oh yes, they are named accurately. 'Jonjishalan', the only sounds they make other than some whines and grunts."

"They did not attempt to kill you?" Illyich asked.

"No, and I think it was because they only kill what they encounter at that moment. They had found me earlier when they weren't on the move."

"So if we attack, we will take fewer losses if they are not chanting 'shalan'?" General Sandovar asked, not to be upstaged by Illyich's inquiries.

"Yes, but I'm afraid that by the time we encounter them—if they cross the strait—they will be chanting that," Rilann replied. "They keep moving west, and they can swim well, as we know, from the last invasion."

"How long do we have?" the king asked.

"That I cannot estimate. I wish I could. I took the liberty of going to the Kilgari to buy more horses." He looked at Captain Illyich who nodded approval. "They will be bringing them down; they were a couple days behind me. They were able to spare three hundred or so. Culls mostly, they wouldn't risk the good stock, of course."

"How many Jonji did you see?"

"Hundreds, I traveled up and down the coast as much as I could. I don't know how deep inland they were though. We could be looking at thousands."

"Thousands!" Sandoval and Illyich exclaimed together.

"I know. They seem to group together, more in hives than what we would call a village, so it was hard to get an accurate count. We need more horses than what I could purchase, but that's the best I could do. By the way, they're expecting payment on delivery."

Captain Illyich spoke then, "With your permission, Sire, we'll go out to meet them and bring them in. We may be able to gather more at the outlying farms in lieu of coin tax. May I have permission to withdraw the sums needed for the Kilgari purchase?"

"Yes, yes of course," the king replied, waving him away.

He turned to Rilann, "So you are sure they will cross and attack?"

"I can't be positive, but the coast is vulnerable. I swam it at the narrowest point before I headed north. I got to shore without anyone noticing. Sentries will need to be posted—manning the towers is essential."

"Sandovar?"

"Yes, Sir."

"We'll need the lookout towers manned and fire signals set up. There's no time to waste," the king continued.

Sandovar saluted and hurried out.

"Sit, Rilann," the king said, indicating a chair.

"Thank you, Sire." Rilann slipped into a padded chair.

"Okay, you can dispense with the formalities,"

Rilann smiled. "I have more news for you."

"Oh really, what?"

"Something more personal."

"Oh, I am intrigued! Wait, bring the wine over."

Rilann rose and retrieved two glasses and a bottle of Castabal Tinto. He poured the shimmering liquid into goblets, and they savored its sweet, rich taste for a moment before Rilann asked, "Do you know of a Lumerian Bard by the name of Heron Hollinghast?"

"Can't say as I have. Hollinghast... Don't they own Holling Mines in Langwer? Eversilver?"

"That's them. Well, he was traveling with a certain paladin, Reist D'Arcannon."

"Ugh." The king made a disgusted face. "D'Arcannons. The curse of the Castillos."

"I suppose we can't blame your sister's fate on all the D'Arcannons."

The king sighed. "I suppose not. It would be easier though. Wait, don't they own a mine, too?"

"Yes. Darcon Iron."

"Oh yes, how could I forget that? So, what about them?"

"They were traveling together with a young girl they were trying to pass off as a boy. She looked to be the—ah, right age as your missing niece—"

"My niece! You don't think—?" The king sat up and leaned forward.

"I do. There was something very familiar behind the shady spell cast on her. She looks like her father, sad to say, she doesn't have Isabela's brilliant coloring." Rilann knew he was flattering now; the king had that same dark hair and coloring.

"Honey?"

"Yes, hair and skin. And there's more. There was an attack."

"By who?"

"That's the strange part." Rilann leaned forward, resting his arms on the table. "Slinkhounds. On a scent that went straight to the child. I heard Hollinghast curse 'Jaarven' for sending them, just a mutter under his breath. He had to be referring to the Archcanon Jaarven Hilde. Who else would have it in for the princess but the man who orchestrated Isabel's downfall?"

The king sipped his wine thoughtfully while he sifted through this news. "It all makes sense—and doesn't make sense any other way."

Rilann swirled the wine in his glass absentmindedly. "I think she has been found. And there are other oddities. She was riding a Leopard Horse."

"No!" The king exclaimed leaning towards him. "I wasn't sure they were real."

"Oh yes, and she has one—or it has her. It would take a very special girl to attract that kind of magic."

"Indeed! So, my niece may have finally been found? Barbarians, what have they done to that poor girl, I wonder? The lost princess of Taivasta. Well, how about that! That will shake things up in New Saar."

Rilann let him think about that for a while. He waited while the king ruminated on all his news. Better it be the king's suggestion than his.

"I suppose we should ask Taivasta for assistance with these damn creatures you tell me about, whatever they are."

"The Jonji?" Rilann asked as if he hadn't thought of it already.

"Yes. It won't be long before they work their way up through the pass if they do cross over the strait. Why should we bear the whole burden? I need you to ride north and ask Sterren."

"Of course."

Chapter 15

THE WARNING

"Ol' Natty Crouse, she looked for a rat
But instead she found an inquisitive cat.
The cat chased the rat, and the rat chased a mouse,
And the mouse bit down on Natty Crouse.

Now she's gone stiff, and surely she'll die
And sad it will be, and we will all cry
When standing by we wave goodbye
To a dark-draped hearse as it just gets worse."

-TAIVASTAN FOLK SONG

Everyone was looking at Greylin with questions in their eyes. The crown was in her hand—she wouldn't let it go. She looked around at them. *How am I going to explain this? Well, first thing, stand up, so I won't feel so much like a child.*

Greylin rose to her feet. The entire settlement had been looking for her. Now they crowded around waiting for her explanation. Hollinghast had his hands on his hips in an uncharacteristic pose. D'Arcannon looked grim and relieved at the same time.

"So," she started, which came out like a croak. "So," she tried again, and it sounded more like a word. "First of all, I am fine now. The Crown is powerful and somewhat dizzying, but I suffered no hurt from the climb or descent or...uh...from the dragon."

She looked around to see how the news was being received. Same curious eyes. A few open mouths. Some were looking into the distance to see if they could still get a glimpse of the dragon.

"Why did you take the Elder Crown?" Koren asked, his voice rising above the rest. The obvious question.

What would be the best answer? She wondered. *Because I wanted it? Because I was obsessed with it and had to have it? That's not even the half of it.*

"Because it is mine," she finally said. "I hid it here for myself centuries ago in another life." *Did that sound as ridiculous to them as it just did to me?* She paused. "It's not just the Elder Crown. It's called the Crown of the Crescent Moon."

Hollinghast's mouth dropped open. D'Arcannon smirked, leaned back, crossed his arms, beamed approval, and chuckled. Finn looked like he wasn't sure whether he should believe her or be impressed that she was telling such a spectacularly creative lie to get out of trouble. The most interesting reaction was from the *shinwazoko* who all went into a huddle and whispered to each other.

It must have been the right answer because Koren approached her, bowed, and said, "Then it is yours. The dragon was here to protect it. He could only allow the true bearer to take it. Then he was free to go home which he has apparently done. How did you bring it here in the first place?"

She frowned, "I didn't see that. I only saw myself placing it. There must have been another dragon. Hmmm, why didn't I see that?"

They looked at her blankly.

"I suppose I could use it again to see if I can find out. However," she looked at her friends, "it packs a powerful punch. I'll need support from either side of me, so I don't fall over. And I might be sick." She blushed with embarrassment. She did not want to be sick in front of everyone.

Sato stepped forward then. "I think I have just the place. When would you like to begin?"

"Oh, right now! I feel that there is an urgency…there is something I haven't seen that I need to."

"Then follow me." Sato motioned to her.

Sato led Greylin to a small meditation room where there was a cushioned chair surrounded by piles of mats. It would be hard to fall and hurt herself there. Sato brought some shell bowls to place nearby, presumably in case she got sick, and others with fresh water in them and a cloth. She was well prepared!

Greylin pronounced it "perfect" and clasped Sato's hands in gratitude. Then she reached for her friends. She asked Hollinghast to stand behind her because he was tall enough to reach over the chair, place the crown on her head, and keep her from falling forward. D'Arcannon she put on her left and Finn on her right. They were to hold her hands once the crown was placed.

Greylin leaned back and relaxed. She wanted to know three things: How she had placed the crown where it was, how to get off the island, and if there was something the crown wanted to tell her, something she felt demanding her attention more and more as each moment passed. She closed her eyes and Hollinghast slipped the crown over her head.

Maybe it was because she was so prepared, or maybe it was because she knew what to expect and could take control, but she wasn't flattened this time. She waited for it, but the effects seemed to hover, waiting for her. She formed the thought *how did I bring the crown here?*

She saw a quick—almost too quick—vision of a large female dragon flying above a small ship with a single gold-colored sail, a boat so small it could hold only one person. A young male dragon flew behind the larger one. They came to the island and the female dragon flew her up to the cave to place the crown, then down again to explain her plan to the people. The vision was gone in a blink of an eye, almost as if the crown didn't want to tell her but was compelled to. *Well, perhaps an easier question, how can we get off this island?*

Different pathways spread away, it felt like she was racing down corridors. The way north to Lumenvalo was a dead end: a raft that sinks and no ship to save them. Here was Castabal (she thought), again, a dead end. She could see them sinking. Here was Sessirra, a raft, a platform of sorts on a whale's back, Finn was leading the whale. They make it to the harbor. Other boats come to the rescue. *That is the path: Finn must find a whale, and we must build a platform or raft out of what scraps we can gather from the shoreline. We can make it!*

Once her mind was settled on a plan, she found her view soaring high above all Allanda. The sight was fascinating. She wasn't sure where she was, but the crown seemed to respond to that immediately and took her over the farm she had worked with Daara, orienting her to Maddy Sedge. She strained to see any sight of Daara or the animals, but the view sped too quickly over the village and southeast to water again, and she assumed, if she understood the maps she had seen in the library at Old Saar correctly, that they were in Castabal, then across the water. The earth was moving, bubbling up and shifting. Her vision drew closer to reveal tall six-legged creatures moving in large groups. *The Jonjishalan,* she thought. *They're real.*

There were thousands of them swarming over the land, making it look like it was moving. They did not resemble anything human. Some were walking on two legs, some on all fours, some even running on six. They were relentless, deterred by nothing. They swam across the narrowest part of the water. Soldiers were fighting them. The slaughter was horrendous yet still they came. Bodies piled up but nothing gave them the slightest pause. They kept coming and eventually overwhelmed the soldiers. The monsters were chanting "shalan, shalan, shalan" in a whispering, moaning tone. Some of the soldiers were on foot, some were on horseback. All of them were being overrun by the onslaught.

She realized that this scene was from only one corridor. She looked down another where she was riding Roki into battle, holding her sword on high and wearing black armor. Reddish colors behind her streaked the vision. Her friends were behind her with many others: Lumerians, Mazarines, and soldiers wearing golden livery. The Jonjishalan stopped. There was something about seeing her that made them veer away. Sparks flew from her sword, and the Jonji began chanting "jonji" instead of "shalan".

She looked around to see when this might occur. Far behind the battle a field of corn was being harvested and put into *kuhilas*, or stooks as some called them. That would be soon for the corn was almost ripened. There was no time to waste. She pulled the crown off her head.

"Finn," she shouted. "You've got to find a whale to get us home!"

Chapter 16

LEVIATHAN

*"The songs of the whales speak to the longing
in a seaman's heart."*

-LOG BOOK ENTRY OF CAPTAIN SKERRY REED

Everyone stared at her as though she had lost her mind. Somehow, she had to convince them that this was real, that there was danger, and no time to lose. She told them what she had seen about the crown and asked, "Koren, can you tell us more about this crown?"

"Ah, well, yes, yes," he hemmed and hawed. "We know of it through our history, our oral history—not much to write on here is there?

"We've been here hundreds of years, and as the story goes, the Elder Queen, the *Akarui Josei,* came to the island on a pretty little ship shaded by a large ice dragon mother and trailed by her smaller son. That's how it is told. She found her way to us by using the crown as a guide. She said it had led her and her people to a safe place, but it also showed her that one day there would be danger and that she had to hide the crown until it would be needed again. The mother dragon carried her up to the cave at the top of the sunwing—for that is what we call the mountain—and the male promised to stay there until she came again. When she did, the dragon would recognize her and let her take the crown.

"Since that is exactly what has happened, we can only assume..." he trailed off in confusion. He and most of the others had stopped believing the tale over the many hundreds of years. Faced with it now, they had to concede to its truth, but they teetered on the edge of disbelief, as did her companions.

"Did she tell you how the crown worked?" Greylin asked.

"She said that it could show the past and the future," Koren answered

"Did she say that it lied?" Greylin asked in a more demanding tone.

"No, no, only that it showed more than one path of things to come."

Greylin stood up and faced her companions. She held the crown in front of her.

"This shows what the outcome will be of any path we choose. You are welcome to test it yourself. What I have seen tells me that I—we—must go to Castabal with all the speed we can muster, and with as much help as we can gather along the way."

Hollinghast held out his hand. She knew he would not be able to resist. His curiosity would pull him to it like a moth to a flame. She motioned to him to sit and handed him the crown.

"Be prepared, it can be dizzying," she cautioned him. "Focus on where I should be—or where we should be—when we leave here."

Hollinghast looked at her meaningfully and nodded. She placed the crown on his head, and he fell backward against the support.

If Hollinghast was having trouble, she would pull the crown off, but it was hard to tell. She decided to try to wait it out without panicking. He was well versed in the ways of magic; he should be able to handle it.

She breathed a sigh of relief when he reached up and took it off. He was pale, and a little shaky. "I see," was all he said.

Another moment or two went by. He rubbed his face with his hands and hummed a spell, probably to clear his head. He looked at Greylin, then at Finn.

"She's right. We've got to get off this island, and you have to be the one to find us transport. A leviathan, I think. There's a lot of us. Including the horses. And then—"

"—we have to go to Castabal," Greylin said.

"—we have to go to Castabal," he said at the same time.

And at the same time again they both said, "There's no time to lose."

Hollinghast rose and turned to their hosts, "Thank you so much for all you have done. A matter of great urgency calls us. If you could supply us with food for our journey, we would be most grateful. We must ready ourselves."

"We are more than happy to help. What do you need?" Koren asked.

Preparations began immediately. The islanders packed fruit and vegetables, many that would keep for a few days. Then they were guided to a wide cave that led straight to the shore without having to scale the cliff to go back the way they came.

The horses weren't where they left them, but Greylin sent a mental picture to Roki and knew they would return soon, cavorting in their joy to see their riders again. In the meantime, the group gathered every scrap of twig, leaf, and driftwood—anything that would float—and bound it all together with twine that the shinwazoko supplied. Small bundles were tied together to make larger bundles until they had a floating platform. It was hardly seaworthy, but it was a firm enough base to ride atop a leviathan.

Meanwhile, Finn had gone through the agony of wearing the crown to locate one of the giant whales called leviathans. He had to lie down a moment or two before swimming off, but he had determined a likely direction. It was near dark when the raft was finished, and Finn arrived with the leviathan. They would have to push the raft out to where the great whale could rise up beneath it, and then get on. They decided to put the horses on first, hoping it wouldn't sink, then climb up later.

They were saying goodbye to a few of the young *Shinwazoko* who volunteered to help when Rilah appeared carrying a bundle under her arm and one slung to her back. "I am going with you," she announced. "I want to find my brother. Like him, I want to know what is out there. My parents have given me their blessing."

They were dumbfounded. No one had seen this coming. *Remember that when you use the crown,* Greylin told herself. *It won't show you everything. There may still be surprises!* She hadn't seen Rilah, but thinking back to her vision, she realized there may have been five shapes sitting on the raft. She just hadn't taken note of it at the time.

"Well," Hollinghast looked at the companions. "We don't have time to argue. Do any of you object?"

Everyone shook their heads "no". Hollinghast and D'Arcannon exchanged looks, shrugged, and laughed a little but said nothing.

"Then, so be it," Hollinghast nodded to Rilah.

The horses did not like the raft idea, especially as it started slowly sinking once they were all on it, nor did they like their riders swimming along beside them in the open sea, but they held. They weren't about to be left behind so they accepted it as the only alternative. Finn was underwater guiding the leviathan.

Slowly, so slowly, Finn brought the beast to the surface. If it rose too fast, the raft would simply slide off its back with the rush of water. Soon Hollinghast was standing rather than swimming, then D'Arcannon. They were able to hold the raft in place so the rest of them could climb on and settle down. The raft was oblong but dwarfed by the expanse of the leviathan's back. Once situated, safe and secure, the great water beast began to swim. To say that it was terrifying to be in deep water again, in the growing darkness, with a huge creature rising beneath them was to minimize what they were all feeling, but the slight back-and-forth sway wasn't unpleasant, and their anxiety began to ease.

Greylin sat between Roki's front legs, Hollinghast and Merelda next to her, and D'Arcannon behind them, keeping Bane calm—he had started to stamp at one point, and they were afraid his giant feet would destroy the raft before they got going. Finn was on top of the leviathan near its head. Rilah sat by herself at the front of the raft, enraptured by the sight of the sea all around her.

"So," Hollinghast said to Greylin, "you have the Sword and now you have the Crown. What do you make of that?"

She was quiet for a while, trying to sum up all that was occurring so fast.

"You want to know if I know, or agree, with what you think has happened," she said.

"Essentially, yes."

"I know…or maybe I should say first that I think I am her, the Hiildan Queen. I have her memories. I now have the Sword and the Crown. Those were hers. She left them—or rather she hid them—so that they could be found later. The only person who could find them would be her because she hid them so well. But how I wound up here, on this island, in this time, I do not understand."

"Do you not know that ELIEL plays a part in our lives?" Hollinghast asked softly.

Greylin was quiet again.

Then she said, "My words make me sound as if I am so full of myself. Who am I to pretend to be so important?"

"You're not pretending, are you?"

"No! But…" she sighed. "So, I am her, in the flesh now, but still as myself. The Hiildan Queen returns as the Princess of Taivasta. You would think one lifetime like that would be enough!"

Chapter 17

RETURN OF THE LOST

All things will work together for good for those who follow the Light of ELIEL.

- THE BOOK OF RETURNS
CREDITED TO ST. RAUNA

They glided through a dark sea for a night and a day and another night. The great tail of the leviathan rocked them back and forth as he swam, and they slept under a canopy of stars by night and shielded themselves from the sun as best they could by day. At noon on the second day they were in sight of land and approached the entrance to Pearladen Bay and the city of Sessirra.

The whale desired to leave and as soon as a nearby ship hailed them, he brought them swiftly to its side. The raft barely held together till the horses were hoisted aboard a vessel smaller than the *Windracer*. The horses hated it, Bane especially, but there was no other way. The raft was starting to deteriorate and would not hold their weight all the way into the bay, and it was a far swim. As soon as the horses were on board, the leviathan descended into the depths and departed.

Once on dry land again, it was tempting to kneel down and kiss the ground, and Greylin now understood why people did that, but there was no time to waste. Finn inquired about the *Windracer* and his cousin Captain Skerry. He was relieved to learn that the captain and crew had made it to safety with the help of whales that guided them to another ship. They thought Finn and his friends had been lost and were ecstatic to see them once again.

Hollinghast and D'Arcannon went to their chapter houses to plead for assistance in Castabal. Greylin decided she would plead her case before the people of Sessirra and she presented herself to Mayor-Council Môr Perlog to request a meeting at the Merchant Hall. To his credit, he held his questions back, and set the meeting for the following evening.

Greylin and Rilah were given rooms at the Cloud House, a villa next to the Merchant Hall reserved for guests and dignitaries. After freeing the North Bay of the Oarman, the Sessirrans agreed that Greylin qualified for special treatment. They were each welcome to take rooms, but Finn chose to stay at home with his mother, and Hollinghast and D'Arcannon stayed at their respective halls.

Rilah and Greylin had most of the next day to themselves while they waited for the meeting. Over a lovely meal of *fisal* and shellfish, Greylin told Rilah the whole story of her battle with the Oarman, her upbringing in Maddy Sedge, and the events that kept sweeping her away from reuniting with her father, King Sterren of Taivasta.

Rilah told Greylin about day to day life on the island. They discovered a mutual love of sewing, and Greylin proudly displayed her pivot scissors which impressed Rilah greatly. Rilah expressed no interest in sword fighting but a keen desire to learn to read and write in the common tongue. Greylin promised to be her teacher.

There was not enough time to tour the city but as the Cloud House was named for its prominence high on the southern cliffs beside the bay, Greylin could point out locations to Rilah as they sat on the veranda. Rilah was not as interested in the sea and the shore in the way Greylin had been when she first arrived in Sessirra. Rilah had seen much of island shores and the wide sea. What she was most fascinated with were things made of metal, carved and inlaid wood of varieties she had never seen before, brightly colored ceramics, elaborate fabrics, and chiseled stone of which there had been next to nothing on the island. She went from one item to another, touching vases, examining trinket boxes, fingering the drapes, and staring at paintings an inch from her nose.

All too soon it was time to prepare to speak to the Sessirrans.

"One more thing," Rilah said.

"What is that?" Greylin asked.

Rilah went to one of the two bundles she had carried all the way from the Isle of Edda and pulled out a robe. "I wanted to give you a gift for letting me come with you. I think it will fit you. You really shouldn't be addressing a city in sailor shorts and a shirt with cut sleeve ends! Try this on."

Greylin held it up. It was a woven, sand-colored dress made of soft flax and decorated with tiny, gleaming shells along the collar and sleeves. It had a wide skirt split at the sides, which covered a pair of narrow pants that would make for easy riding on Roki. Greylin's mouth dropped open in astonishment.

"Rilah, this is beautiful. I don't know what to say."

"I had a feeling you needed me as much as I need you. Go ahead. Try it on."

Greylin tore off the Sessirran shirt and shorts and slipped on the dress and pants. Then she buckled on her sword. Rilah pulled her over to a long mirror.

"Well now, there's someone they might listen to!" Greylin exclaimed.

Rilah laughed. "Let's hope so. Now, let me tame this hair."

***

While Greylin and Rilah were making preparations, D'Arcannon was once again seated in front of Commander Rufter. He had been ushered in with considerable rapidity given the redundant security checks of the Palonen Hall. D'Arcannon stifled the desire to bounce his right leg up and down in rapid impatience.

"I am most pleased to see you among the living!" Rufter exclaimed. "I thought we were going to be a paladin short."

"I am most pleased myself," D'Arcannon replied.

"Report. And leave nothing out."

D'Arcannon relayed his adventures from the moment they embarked on the *Windracer* to the moment of sitting before the Commander.

Hollinghast, in turn, was relaying the same tale to Master Hugh D'Haas, but while D'Arcannon would report the facts without conjecture, Hollinghast's emphasis veered toward the confirmation of what Master Ashrut Longten was studying so intently in the lower levels of the Library of Saar. The mysterious disappearing island of Edda was in fact a downed flying ship. The people who dwelt there claimed this with matter-of-fact certainty. There was, in his opinion, no intent to fool anyone with this tale because they had no desire to encounter anyone in the outer world.

His other news was the startling confirmation that the Second Arcanum had been found in the form of the Crown of the Crescent Moon. The Valkoinen had never known what the Second Arcanum would be, only that there was one, as well as a third. The fact that events had conspired to bring this discovery about just as they had done with the First Arcanum was evidence of a greater hand at work in the destinies of the people of Allanda.

Chapter 18

THE GOLDEN BRIGADE

*"There are times when you will find help
where you least expect it."*

- THE BOOK OF RETURNS
CREDITED TO ST. RAUNA

Hollinghast was speaking to the Lumerians, and D'Arcannon to the Mazarines. Greylin alone would face the citizens of Sessirra and ask for their help. She was curious as to how many would show up. Town Criers had been announcing the meeting throughout the day. To her surprise, the Merchant Hall was packed. The people of Sessirra were still curious to see the lady who had defeated the monstrous Oarman and been cast ashore, and returned, from the mysterious vanishing island that many had thought was just a myth.

As Greylin looked out over a sea of faces, she asked herself what in the world she was thinking to be in this place at this time. *What if I lose my voice again?*—but there was no time to think—she had to shake off any thoughts about all those people staring at her.

"Thank you for coming," she began and found to her great delight that she could speak, and that sound traveled well and strongly throughout the room so that she would not have to shout. "And thank you all for your generosity toward me." This was greeted with thunderous applause and "No, no, thank YOU's" all around.

"You know me as the Golden Pearl. I am she who returned to rid you of the ruination of your trade, your lives, and your freedom from the monster known as the

Oarman. In doing so, I claimed this sword." She stopped there and pulled out the sword and raised it above her head. "It was hidden years ago in anticipation of the need to free the people of Sessirra. One that I could not anticipate, and by a path I could not see; yet ELIEL guided my steps here to make good on a promise that held for hundreds of years." She hesitated, *I forgot to check on that, how many years was it? Oh drat, who cares? Keep going.*

"I mean to keep that promise. I pledge this sword to the protection of the people of Sessirra." There was a lot of cheering at this point which was a great relief.

"And now Sessirra faces a new threat." That made them nervous and a hush fell over the crowd.

She sheathed her sword and pointed to the east.

"I have seen by the Grace of ELIEL that guided me here—" Good time to pause and let that sink in. *If I tried to explain the Crown, they'll never get it. Just skip the how and go to the what.*

"—that far from these shores a new menace looms. Sessirra is not in danger at this very moment, but Castabal is, and then it will spread through Taivasta, and finally, lastly, to Sessirra. This has happened before, and Sessirra was spared. My deepest desire is for Sessirra to be spared once more so that the beauty of this city will not be destroyed but will continue to grow and prosper."

Big cheer. "Prosper" was always a key to the hearts of merchants.

"You have heard of this threat. They swarm like a plague, kill without hesitation, and devour without conscience: the Jonjishalan." This caused a stir. Everyone started talking at once. Greylin let them get worked up.

"Please, please," she called, but her voice was not strong enough to shout over them. Finally, she raised her sword again and waited until they quieted.

"Tomorrow my friends and I ride to Castabal to head off this invasion. I know I ask a lot. These invasions have not started yet, and you have heard no news of it before now, but if we wait, it will be too late. This I have seen.

"I have no right to ask you to follow me, but I will welcome any who choose to do so. We have no armaments for you, no horses, and no supplies. These you must provide for yourselves, for your own protection, for the city of Sessirra, for your wives and children.

"If you bear any love for me, any gratitude for the liberation of the North Bay—which I have just been told has been renamed the Golden Bay in my honor, and I must say, truly, I am honored—then please meet me on the shores of eastern Castabal where the scourge advances even now. There is no time to lose. I must ride. And I pray that you follow swiftly. *Sessirra must stand.*"

There was thunderous cheering. The Mayor-Council, the man who had gifted Greylin with the scabbard which now encased the Sword Argente, approached her and took her hands. He agreed to oversee the formation of those who volunteered.

Thank ELIEL, she breathed, after thanking him profusely, for that would be a task that would take too much time—just to find the resources for supplies—and she had to leave tomorrow. She had little hope that much could be mustered on such short notice, but she had to ask.

How wrong she was!

When she left Cloud House the next morning, over five hundred men, mounted and armed, were waiting for her. She knew that Sessirra might have an armed force, but she had never seen them and assumed that they relied on the Mazarines to keep order. Behind the mounted men were light wagons already stocked. Sessirra was a rich city, so much so that supplies were no problem; all that was needed was to load them up. They must have worked all night to prepare them. Whether they could keep up with the riders remained to be seen, but they were ready to depart.

The well-built, heavily muscled man with a scar on his cheek introduced himself as captain of the guard and approached on her his horse, saluted, and said, "My lady, we are at your service if you will accept us. We have been released from our sworn duty to the people of Sessirra to accompany you and swear to your service. I am Captain Everlan Redmond. If it pleases you, we have chosen to call ourselves the Golden Brigade."

Greylin was speechless, a lump filled her throat. Perhaps too long because the horses snorted and stamped after a while, and Roki let loose with a high and long whinny which was a rallying cry to the horses as they all answered at once. *What do I say?* She wondered frantically. She had to pull deep on old memories. She tried to speak but nothing came out and she gestured a thank you. That seemed to release her voice.

"Captain Redmond, I accept your offer and extend to you and your men the greatest gratitude. My heart is full." She got on Roki at this point to get high enough to see them all. She cleared her throat and took a deep breath.

"Men of the Golden Brigade! Do you swear to be true, faithful, brave, and steadfast in your service?"

Hollinghast had arrived behind her and sizing up the situation played lightly on his kantelyre and sang a word that enabled her voice to carry, so much so it startled her at first.

They answered, "we do" and "aye" and "yes" in unison.

"If we are successful in our venture, I will release you from your vows so that you may return to whatever life you choose. Your oath does not come before your oath to king and country but only to support this venture in defense of the whole of Allanda.

"However, I will reveal to you that you are sworn to the Princess Cianalas Hilde of Taivasta and that even though this claim has not been proved or accepted yet as legal, your oath can be made with a clear conscience. Please present your weapon and place them over your hearts."

Some pulled swords, some axes, and some polearms and pikes.

"Do you swear your allegiance to me as your leader for this venture?"

Again, each answered positively, each in his own way.

"Be assured that I will be as wise and courageous a leader as ELIEL may grant. I swear that I will not lack in resolve nor risk your lives rashly, nor will I spare my own blood in the accomplishment of our mission. Allanda must stand!"

Once again, they cheered, and she could see the light of loyalty in their eyes. She turned to begin the ride to Castabal and Roki neighed his rallying cry once more. The horses responded, deep-toned horns were sounded, and they set off.

Hollinghast was followed by a small group of Lumerian Singers, and D'Arcannon approached with a cohort of thirty Mazarine knights.

Let me treasure this day, she thought, *for darker days may come.*

Chapter 19

RILANN FAILS

"A great man is nobody in another man's castle."

-A TRAGEDY IN THREE ACTS
BY THE BARD OF MADHIA

Rilann Blake was sitting on a bench outside the antechamber to the King of Taivasta's throne room. His papers had been presented and despite his protestations of urgency, he was relegated to the bench of petitioners without any preference. He was controlling his temper, but barely. Sunlight poured through long windows behind him and he was feeling uncomfortably warm. He wondered if the design was accidental or purposeful.

Finally, the doors were opened, and they were allowed into the throne room. They jostled for position and Rilann tried to push ahead but a surly guard with a pike barred his way. The room was long, columned, and reminded Rilann more of a church than anything else. Seats, like pews were arranged on either side beside the columns. The floor in the middle was open, however, so those requesting a hearing had to stand. He glanced at those sitting on either side. They were from all walks of life and he realized that this was entertainment for them.

The king sat on a raised throne at one end. His current queen, Lyda, was on his right, and Archcanon Jaarven Hilde on his left. Behind stood two guards at attention. In front on either side stood two others. Tall windows colored in red, white, green & blue representing the Four Orders rose loftily behind him. Along each side, high above, smaller panes of leaded stained glass told stories of Queen Hiilda and St. Rauna.

I should have come with a retinue, he thought. *I am getting no recognition for the status of my mission. I came quickly on my own, as I often travel, but this barbarian king has no manners.*

Impatiently, he waited through a case of land encroachment by a farmer sneakily moving fences over onto church land (remove them at once), charges of heresy against a group near the desert who claimed St. Rauna was a man (execute them—Rilann shuddered—*truly? They do that here?*), and a request from the Archcanon Jaarven that he be provided with an elite guard to seek out other heretics (granted). Finally, it was Rilann's turn.

"Your majesty," he bowed and tried to keep the irritation out of his voice. "I come on an urgent mission from King Castillo in Castabal. The Jonjishalan are on the move in the eastern lands, soon to begin another expansion into Castabal. King Castillo requests assistance according to the Articles of Agreement signed at the end of the Jonjishalan wars."

The King Sterren looked at him thoughtfully. "I believe those Articles apply only if the Jonjishalan actually cross the Strait of Tammerlin. There is no obligation to mount such an expensive expedition on a hunch that they *might* do so. What do you base this on?"

Rilann explained his capture and observations.

"So. You *think* they *might.* And what in your vast experience qualifies you for this assessment? You certainly weren't here the last time it happened, you're far too young."

Rilann flushed with anger. If this was the tactic Sterren was taking, how could he circumvent it?

"But your majesty, they are already on the move. They travel to the west as far as the eye can see!"

Archcanon Jaarven intervened at this point, "And could just as easily stop at the water's edge or turn around. This is supposition without proof. We should empty the garrisons of New Saar on the word of this man? It would be a fine thing to let our enemies know that New Saar has no protection!"

"Perfectly true!" the king agreed. "If they do cross and begin an advance, I will honor our agreement. Until then, do not bother me with bad dreams." And with that, King Sterren waved him away with a dismissive gesture, arose and left the room.

Enemies? Rilann pondered. *Who are these enemies he speaks of?* He looked at the Archcanon, *What fears does that man pour into the king's head?*

Chapter 20

RIMMON

"Rimmon is a land characterized by its plenitude of water. Everywhere there are rivers, streams, rivulets, fountains, ponds, lakes, and irrigation canals. To say that it is a rich and fertile land is to understate the wealth the water brings to its gardens."

- WATERMAN GREEN, MASTER GARDENER

It was over five hundred miles to the capital city of Rimmon in Castabal, and that was if an arrowswift was flying directly there. The Golden Brigade tried to ride as swiftly, but there were obstacles that had to be avoided, particularly the Letto Fens to the east of Sessirra which could swallow a wagon in less than a minute, so a detour to the southwest was necessary. After that, they swung to the east to avoid the dry Kilgarin desert, and only then could there be a clear run through the Plains of Dolor.

The Golden Brigade did not slow their progress as much as Greylin feared they might, and they made good headway. She was grateful for the company of her friends but made it a point to visit with Captain Redmond and the other soldiers in camp. Every night, no matter how weary the men were, after they had eaten and settled, the kanteles, drums, and fiddles came out and strains of "Evie's Polka" and "Sailing Up the Bay" ended each evening on a happy note. She was surprised at how young some of the recruits were, but the older ones brushed off her inquiries with, "it's good experience for 'em."

One evening she came upon Capt. Redmond sitting alone by a campfire and joined him. He rose and saluted but she waved him back down and sat near.

"Sleep as we near a battle does not come easily," he said, settling back on a camp chair.

"It does not," she agreed.

"They say death is a part of life. I disagree. Grief is part of life. Fear of the loss caused by death is a part of life. Those are the things one must face. Grief and fear. Death is nothing in itself, only an absence."

Greylin sat quietly, listening and mulling over his words.

He continued, "Some of us will die in the coming battle, but we will die together. It is those left behind who I pity."

"I hope you are not one of them," she said in a soft voice.

"If I am, know that I have no regrets for joining this cause. I only ask that whatever I have or am due, please make sure that my wife and children receive it."

"I will do it myself if I am still alive when this is finished."

Redmond nodded, satisfied.

"Good luck, my friend," she said as she rose to continue her visits with others.

* * *

Thanks to Rilah's wisdom to buy yards of gold-colored cloth before they left Sessirra, Greylin and Rilah were able to make uniforms for each other and Finn to match the brigade. There were a few yards left over and Greylin chose to make banners. She needed a symbol on the banners and decided on two overlapping circles pierced by an upright sword. There wasn't much time for fine embroidery on the road, especially since she spent each night clapping and singing with the brigade, so a simple design was chosen.

To inspire her troops, for that is how she thought of them now, she brought out the items she had been hiding since Daara entrusted them to her which seemed a very long time ago in the cottage in Maddy Sedge. Her mother's rings now adorned her fingers. She hoped they would disperse any doubts that she might not be who she claimed to be.

It hardly mattered, however, to the Golden Brigade. They had seen the corpse of the Oarman and that was enough for them. As for Hollinghast, he merely raised an eyebrow and said, "You are full of surprises." D'Arcannon smiled and said nothing. She had the feeling that he had already made up his mind, though as to what exactly, she wasn't sure.

Rilah simply smiled, but Finn said that if all else failed, she could sell the rings and live a luxurious life. When she asked him where that might be if the Jonjishalan swarmed over Allanda, he just shrugged his shoulders and gave her a sheepish grin.

"There are still other places in this world," he replied with his calm smile. "Selkans sail farther than humans would."

"Where?" Greylin demanded, but he did not answer.

***

Hollinghast alerted the other chapter houses of the Lumerians about the imminent Jonji invasion with messages sent by arrowswifts to New Saar, Madhia, and Langwer. D'Arcannon had done the same, only through horsemen sent to Mazarine strongholds. They, in turn, would request healers from the Viridian order, for it would go without saying that there would be injuries and casualties.

"So," she said to Hollinghast as they rode along one day, "when did you suspect that I was the Hiildan Queen returned?"

"Well, you know, that is why we went to Saar—Old Saar that is—so that I could look at the records. Queen Hiilda wrote in her journals that she would leave three gifts for herself. The Lumerians have waited for many years. We call them the Three Arcanum."

"Three? That's right, you said that when we were leaving Saar. I remember now. What was the third?"

Greylin wondered how she could have possibly forgotten that.

"She called it the Chalice Rose."

"Where is it?"

He laughed, "Where were any of them? Only you know."

"Sorry!" She laughed, too. "You're right. What does it do?"

"I don't know that either," he answered.

"You suspected from the beginning?"

"I began to suspect when you expressed your desire for a sword, and for training. How can I impress upon you how unusual that is? You have yet to meet any of the women of the court. Then I watched you. You have a certain innate skill. I knew there were three items hidden, and I knew one was a sword. How would the Hiildan Queen acquire it? She would have to want it. She would have to know deep down that it waited for her. It is one of the most powerful magic items in the world, attuned to one person only. Its call would be maddening. And this I saw in you. So I decided to look further and thus our side trip occurred. What happens then? You acquire a horse that is in itself a magical creature. More than you know, there are still things we do not know about Roki here. And let's see, what happened then?"

He leaned over and looked at her.

She laughed. "We got shipwrecked on a traveling, disappearing island, and I find the Crown of the Crescent Moon and ride another magical creature down an ice mountain."

"Correct. Got it in one. As if I didn't already know by then! But you know what clinched it?" He chuckled.

"What?"

"When you came down the mountain, you started taking charge. From that moment on, I was following you and not the other way around."

Greylin blushed. "Oh my, I hadn't noticed."

"It comes naturally to you. If we had any doubt—"

"We?"

"Reist and I. When you started sounding like his Aunt Rhemet, he knew exactly who you were. I think deep down he knew it instinctively before me."

She laughed again. "I didn't mean to be bossy."

"You need to be. Look, you have a whole army behind you. Someone has to tell them what to do."

Greylin grimaced. "I suppose, but that's something that worries me."

"Why?"

"I didn't see Rilah when I wore the crown. She wasn't in the picture. What if I missed something else?"

"I think the Crown shows us the main path to take, but at each moment it may change and change again. Perhaps it's time to wear it once more to allay your concerns."

Greylin pondered his advice. It made perfect sense, but she loathed putting the crown on again. She hated the dizziness, the speed at which it flew down timelines, the continual clicking of changed direction, and the fear that she would miss something important. *It has to be done though,* she reasoned. *I have pledged myself to this cause and to these men. I owe it to them, surely.*

That night in her tent—for now she and Rilah had a fine tent to call their own courtesy of the Mayor-Council of Sessirra—she decided to try the crown. As before, she placed Hollinghast behind her and Finn and D'Arcannon at either side. Rilah sat at her feet with an empty bowl in case she was sick, and a cup of fresh water as she came out of the seeing. Greylin took a deep breath, leaned back and focused. Hollinghast placed the crown on her head.

Greylin was slammed back again while lights and movement were speeding round at a dizzying rate. She saw the Golden Brigade riding together, banners flying, and then the vision changed. She was in a strange city, the Guard around her. She flashed down another path and was riding with the brigade behind her. With an act of sheer will, she brought herself to the present, right here, right now, and stopped the swirling visions. It was like holding a runaway horse by sheer concentration. She let herself look forward from the present moment to the future of

Castabal. *A horrid slaughter of writing creatures!* She gasped and leaped ahead in time where she was again riding at the head of the Guard, the rest of the brigade following.

She tore the crown off and gasped.

"That is enough," she said enigmatically. "We must stay our course."

***

Three and a half weeks later they rode into Rimmon. It was nearing full summer and Greylin watched the corn anxiously as they rode. Castabal had a warmer climate than Taivasta. An ocean current from the south brought rain and warm weather with it, or so Finn explained. The flowers were in full bloom and corn was ready to be picked in some fields. The vegetation was lush, the birds brightly colored, and tiny lizards darted up the tree trunks and along the rock walls. The travelers would have been delighted with everything if their mission were not so urgent.

They approached Torilinna Castle on a wide road leading up a hill that was flanked on either side with water flowing down a series of long flat steps. There were guards at the gates who managed to look unsurprised by a trail-worn army showing up unannounced. They challenged the travelers and Hollinghast took the lead.

"Greetings. The Princess Cianalas Hilde of Taivasta wishes an audience with her uncle, King Castillo of Castabal along with her companions, the Paladin Reist D'Arcannon, Master Finn Skellig and the Lady Rilah. My name is Master Heron Hollinghast. Behind us are five regiments of the Golden Brigade who have sworn to protect the Princess and defend Allanda from the Jonjishalan."

Greylin noticed a definite eye-bulging from the two guards. To their credit, they did not become more officious from shock but assessing the situation rightly, became extremely polite. The one on the right clicked his heels and bowed. "At once, good Sir. If you would but wait a moment while I announce you."

Hollinghast bowed forward gracefully over Merelda's neck. "Of course."

And so they waited. The guard went to another guard, who called to another guard. Greylin wondered if by the time the news got to the castle, and to her uncle, just who would he be told was at the gates? Something like, "The king's uncle is at the gate with an army and they have a heron with them and a lot of gold." She told this to Finn and Rilah while they were waiting, and they couldn't help giggling at it.

A few minutes later five horseguards rode up to escort them. Greylin so wanted to ask them who they thought everyone was but restrained herself. She asked Captain Redmond to stay behind with the Brigade and was escorted with her four companions to the main entrance. To Greylin's surprise, the king was there himself to greet them.

"Welcome!" he cried. "Is it true that my long-lost niece has just ridden into my courtyard?"

As everyone else stopped, Greylin rode forward and dismounted. She looked deeply into his eyes as he did hers.

"You are the King of Castabal?" she asked.

"The very same," he replied.

Greylin bowed, "Then I am your true niece, the daughter of your sister Isabela. Here is the ring she wore until the day of her death."

She held out her hand to him. His eyes misted as he took her hand and kissed the ring.

"Come in and be refreshed. But first, explain this army, I do not quite believe what I am hearing."

"We are not here for hospitality alone, my uncle, but to bring what aid we may to the threat facing your shores to the east. This is the Golden Brigade, pledged to me, but there are Mazarines as well as Lumerian mages, still to come as well as Viridian healers who are being alerted to travel here from the north."

"How came this to be? Did your father Sterren send you? Why would he risk his daughter now? I do not understand."

"No, no, he does not know. Let us go in, and I will explain."

As they entered Torilinna from the north, a dusty, tired Rilann Blake rode in from the west to the private wing, a picture of discouragement.

Chapter 21

A SURPRISE REUNION

"Long did the princess wait to feel that sense of belonging that most of us feel from birth. I think the meeting with her uncle had a long-term effect upon her sense of self."

- DIARY OF LADY RILAH OF THE ISLAND

King Castillo ushered them into a lavish receiving room. Greylin was suddenly very aware of the fact that they were unwashed and dirty from the road, and probably smelled like horses, leather, and sweat. She declined to sit after one look at the beautifully embroidered couch.

"I think it might be better if we cleaned up first. May we impose on your hospitality? I fear we have arrived rough, trail worn, and weary. What we have to say can wait a little longer."

"Of course! Of course! What was I thinking? Garron will lead you to rooms, and we will have food and drink brought up immediately. Dear Cianalas, may I send someone to assist you?"

"No, Rilah will stay with me if we could have a room that accommodates two."

"As you wish, of course. Dinner will be in two hours—we can discuss our business then if you think that will give you time to refresh?"

"That would be ideal. I cannot thank you enough."

"We can garrison your men as well without difficulty if that is agreeable to you?" he continued.

"You are generous, Uncle."

They all nodded, thanked him, nodded again, and followed Garron, a tall, elegant man who led them out another door.

"I wonder what he makes of all of us," D'Arcannon whispered.

"A small invasion I would think," Hollinghast whispered back.

Two hours later, bathed and combed and dressed in the gown Rilah had brought for her, they followed Garron, who discreetly waited in the corridor for their appearance.

***

Rilann handed his horse to a groom and went to his quarters. His news wasn't good, and he was puzzled by his visit to Taivasta. No time to sort it all out, he wanted to report within the hour to get it off his mind and clear it for the coming battle. He tried to come up with a way to soften the fact that King Sterren had turned him down. Some approach that wouldn't enrage Castillo so he could keep the lines of communication open for another try. If the situation worsened, he was going to have to try again. He could think of nothing more clever than stating the facts and alluding to the oddness of Sterren's behavior.

He strode into the throne room's antechamber an hour later and greeted his king.

"Rilann! I didn't realize you were back."

"I just rode in, m'lord. I'm afraid I don't have good news for you."

"You can't be serious!" The king's mouth dropped open in surprise.

"Sterren will not send any reinforcements to our defense right now. I can't account for it. Something odd was going on there. He seemed to think that either it was some kind of trick to weaken his defenses or that we simply are unable to assess the threat realistically."

"Well, luckily we probably won't need him because we have reinforcements already."

"From where?" Rilann stopped in his tracks.

"You probably won't believe it when I tell you. In fact, they rode in a bit before you. Surprised you didn't meet up with each other."

"I came in from the west. Who are they?"

"From what she tells me, it is my niece the Princess Cianalas, along with the companions you told me about earlier, two others, and a small army including Mazarines and Lumerians mages. They promise that more Mazarines and Lumerians are on the way, independent of Sterren's refusal. Oh, and healers, too."

"How?" Rilann eyes lit up with relief.

"That's what we're going to find out at dinner. Care to join us?"

"Wild horses couldn't keep me away."

"That reminds me, the Kilgarin horses arrived. They look good."

***

Before dinner, Garron led Greylin's party to a cozy gathering room adjacent to the dining room. Here the king introduced everyone to his family in a more relaxed setting. His wife, Queen Vittoria, was holding the newest member of the family, baby Valentin.

The three-year-old daughter, Virdiana, seemingly fascinated by the baby, kept putting her face up to him, making him laugh or sometimes scaring him out of his wits. Vittoria, taking it all in stride, handed the baby off for Greylin to hold, much to her delight. The seven-year-old brother, Lumin, kept ordering Virdiana to stop. There were three others, Darien who was about five who totally ignored the group after giving them a dour stare and saying, "Pleased to meet you".

Serafina was ten, and it was she, Lumin, and Virdiana who crowded about Greylin, Finn, and Rilah, overwhelming them with attention. The oldest and likely heiress to the throne was Romana. She was polite but reserved and never left her father's side.

Serafina, the ten-year-old, wanted to know how Greylin could be a cousin. She had cousins on her mother's side but couldn't understand how Greylin could be one as well. Greylin was at a loss at how to respond to all their questions while dodging Virdiana's persistent pestering of the baby. Virdiana started poking the baby's face and thankfully, Queen Vittoria rescued him before she poked out an eye. Finn handled them well, as did Rilah, both of whom had more experience with children. As overwhelmed as Greylin was with all the attention, she was still heartened to know they were her own family.

My family, she thought, as she took the king's hand to enter the dining room. *I have an actual family!* The enormity of that was staggering. She had been very much alone as a child, except for Daara. She missed Daara terribly even if she was no blood relation, and she hadn't thought about the royal family of Castabal becoming a real family for her. In fact, she hadn't believed she was Cianalas until she wore the Crown. Now to suddenly have relatives, particularly six cousins, was a surprise she hadn't counted on. *I have a place to be if I need it. If things go wrong in New Saar, I have a place to go. Castabal would take me in, I know it.*

The queen's sister, the Lady Serenia, acted as the queen's only lady-in-waiting. She and Hollinghast got into a conversation about the pros and cons of learning the language of magic before learning the magical application of it. Apparently, they agreed.

In Castabal mages were taught the language first; in Taivasta they had dispensed with that for the sake of urgency at some point in the past. Hollinghast and a few others were trying to correct that. What the mages in Taivasta didn't realize was the "fading" that would take place as a result of taking that shortcut. Castabalian mages never faded. Added to that was the acceptance of women mages which Taivasta spurned. The discussion was intense and Greylin had never seen Hollinghast so taken with a woman.

They entered the dining room and Greylin gasped at its beauty. It seemed to be glowing with light. Glass, silver, crystal, and candles all glittered on the white tablecloth. Paintings adorned the walls and flowers filled jeweled vases. Mirrors on the walls reflected the candlelight back and forth endlessly. *This morning,* Greylin mused, *I was sitting on a stool over a campfire.* Even at Cloud House, the meals had been private and simplified. Here at this table, she came face to face with all the social skills she lacked.

Garron managed to get everyone arranged and seated. Greylin, Finn, and Rilah kept their hands in their laps and tried not to look terrified. They watched everyone more keenly than an owl watches a running mouse. D'Arcannon gave them the eye, and they focused on him. He was across from Greylin and realized they had left out an important part of her training in etiquette. She counted on him to lead her through it somehow. Finn was on her right, he was probably ready to pass out from nerves, too, and Rilah was on her left. The three of them were about to fake their way through a formal dinner. Greylin had an almost overwhelming urge to start giggling at the ridiculousness of the whole thing when Rilann Blake walked in.

Rilah rose and stood stock still in shock.

He hadn't noticed her yet and headed to an empty chair at the king's left.

"Rilann! *Anata no imōtodesu!*" she exclaimed.

That stopped him, and his head snapped toward her in shock.

"Who?—How?" He squinted at her. "Rilah?"

She stumbled around her chair and ran to him and threw her arms around him.

"Now who is this young lady, Rilann?" the king asked.

"My-my sister. My twin. I haven't seen her since I— in a long time. Rilah, our parents?" He held her away and looked anxiously into her eyes.

"They are well. I had to leave, Rilann. Like you, I had to see. Our brother, he is still with them. He is happy to stay. I wanted to find you."

They embraced again and Rilann looked at Hollinghast, D'Arcannon, and Greylin. You could see him trying to fit the pieces together.

Finn and Greylin looked at each other and grinned. They were enjoying dinner far more than they thought they would.

The rest of dinner went along happily. The attention was off them because all eyes were on the twins' reunion. There was a change of chairs so that Rilann could sit next to his sister. Finn and Greylin followed D'Arcannon's choice of drink and drank when he drank and ate what he chose and when and picked up the right utensils by watching him. D'Arcannon was his usual charismatic self and would steal attention away from them at critical moments, complimenting the food, the decor, asking if the person sitting next to him would like more of this or that, complimenting the color of his or her garb. It was distracting enough to those around them but also wildly entertaining to watch him work it.

Later, Hollinghast told the story of the Oarman and the gratitude the Sessirrans expressed. He was able to lay on the praise which Greylin wouldn't have been able to do herself. She was surprised that he then went on to tell the whole story of the floating island of Edda. He had the table's full attention which took the burden off D'Arcannon and everyone else. He told them about the Crown of the Crescent Moon and explained why they were arriving with additional troops and assistance.

Rilann jumped in and verified the power of the crown. Greylin had the feeling that he had never admitted to it before—*who would believe him?*—but with the five companions supporting his experience, he was emboldened. The king was so enthralled he forgot to eat.

Chapter 22

TWIN CONFIDANTES

"It's not what you see that trips you up,
it's what you don't see."

-THE MEMOIRS OF QUEEN HIILDA OF SAAR

Later that evening, Rilah and Rilann strolled arm and arm in the fragrant gardens of Torilinna castle. Night-blooming jasmine glowed in the dusk, rivaling the gardenias and roses for color and scent. Fireflies blinked their tiny lights guided by invisible elementals, and nightingales trilled in the shadows.

"Rilah, what made you do such a thing?" Rilann asked.

"I could ask the same of you, brother. Why did you leave?" she countered.

Rilann was silent for a few steps, searching for words of honesty that he had never spoken to anyone before. "I wasn't like everyone else. It wasn't until I came here that I knew why. My heart was never touched by the girls on our island no matter how beautiful they were, yet the boys I found appealing. This was not the way of things. When I came here, I looked upon the young king and my heart was his from that moment."

"Does he—"

"Return my affection? No, not in the way in which he loves his wife, but he cares deeply for me, and that will have to be enough."

"I am sorry, Rilann. I think I understand for I have the same problem in reverse. We are twins and I fear that we somehow switched who we were in the womb. The moment I saw Greylin, I loved her and would not be parted from her. She is not of that inclination, so I, too, suffer the same fate as you."

Rilann stopped and turned to her, holding her by the shoulders. "Rilah, no, not you as well? Is it our fate to suffer so?"

"I fear it is, brother. I cannot stop loving her, but her heart is for another even if she herself does not know it. If it is the same for you, I am grateful that we at least have each other for comfort, what little that may provide."

They embraced and tears flowed for the first time for each of them, easing the pain they had carried in silence and secrecy.

***

Late that evening when Rilah returned, she crept in quietly but Greylin awoke anyway.

"You're back," Greylin announced, stating the obvious.

"Sorry to wake you," Rilah replied, speaking softly as if that would undo the amount of waking that had already been done.

"How is Rilann?" Greylin sat up and pulled one of the satin pillows in front of her to prop her elbows on. They were in a large room with two beds. Lavender wallpaper flocked with gold roses glimmered in the candlelight from two wall sconces. Pale satin sheets covered the beds and draped the tall windows.

Oh no, she wants to talk, Rilah thought. All she wanted was to go to bed and soothe the emotions the talk with her brother had stirred up. Instead she sat on the edge of Greylin's bed.

"He wanted to know all about the people on the island. I wanted to know what he has been doing. He seems happy here."

"Your brother is so handsome," Greylin said. "Is he married?"

"Oh no! Not at all."

"Does he have a girlfriend?"

Rilah started in alarm. "Ah, I—we didn't talk about that." *I just lied,* she thought. *I didn't ever want to lie to her, and I just did. I don't know what to say.* "I think he does," she finally said and hoped that would discourage her.

Greylin's face dropped a little, then brightened. "Can you find out for me?" she asked, undeterred.

"I… sure, sure I will." Rilah paused, thinking furiously how to deflect Greylin's interest. "That D'Arcannon is good looking."

"Reist? He's a paladin, he can't be with anyone."

Rilah turned to her in surprise. "Why not?"

"He would lose his powers. He wouldn't be a paladin anymore. All paladins are like that; that's why there are so few of them," Greylin said, a tinge of regret in her voice.

That explains everything, Rilah thought. "What happens if they do? Does that ever happen?"

"Yes, but they become warrior knights again. He would never be happy."

These people are blind, Rilah thought.

Greylin frowned, irritated though she didn't know why. "Now about tomorrow," she said, changing the subject. "I want you to stay here."

"What? I want to go with you." Rilah protested.

"I talked it over with the king—my uncle. I keep trying to get used to that. His advisers want him here, and he wants Rilann to stay as well. They weren't in my visions so I don't expect anything to go wrong if they stay here. Rilann, of course, will want you to be with him."

"Don't I have a say?"

"If you insist, I wouldn't stop you. But will you be helping me kill these beasts or will you be distracting me with worry about you?"

Rilah got up and walked over to a marble topped washstand. She picked up a china pitcher decorated with painted violets and poured water into a matching bowl and washed her face with scented soap. She took her time, enjoying the luxury thinking over what Greylin had said. Then she jumped backward onto her own bed. This always made Greylin laugh. Rilah would never get over the luxurious beds in grand houses. On the island, people either slept on mats on platforms or in strung hammocks.

"Is Finn going?" she asked.

"Yes. I think he can be useful, and I wouldn't worry about him as much. I don't think he would stay here if I asked him to anyway," Greylin said, easing back onto another pillow.

Rilah thought this over. It seemed unfair, but it was reasonable, and she couldn't find a way to counter it. She was suddenly very tired and didn't feel like talking anymore. She looked over at Greylin and saw to her surprise that her friend had fallen asleep, the pillow still clutched under her arms.

Chapter 23

FRONT LINES

*"When you don your armor,
it's time to harden your heart."*

-SONG OF THE MAZARINE KNIGHTS

The next morning the travelers had a less formal breakfast—it was brought to their rooms—and they turned their thoughts to war. They met in the antechamber of the throne room to look at maps, devise a plan, and organize.

In the middle of tracing a route to the east with her finger on one of the maps, Greylin noticed a guard come through a side door bearing some dark metal. King Castillo had him place it on the table and leave.

"My dear niece, do you think you could fit into this armor?" he asked.

Greylin was astonished. She crossed over to him and looked it over.

"It is armor I wore as a younger man, mine for ceremonial occasions. I hated having to wear it, and it was never necessary. Just show, you know? So uncomfortable in the heat. But it's needed here and now, and you can't be wearing a dress if you insist on going to the front lines. I don't want to lose you now that we finally have you back. My sister would not be pleased."

Until that moment, Greylin's mother was never completely real to her, yet she could tell, and feel, that she had always been a real person for her uncle. She shook off the feelings of loss that threatened to rise within her and picked up the chest piece.

It seemed like it would fit. It had adjustable chainmail on the sides, presumably so that one could get more than a single year's wear out of it. Her only concern was that it would be too long or short, but each piece had been made a bit short with chain mail borders to fill in the gaps and adjust for height. It was blackened which seemed odd, but the king explained that was to make a child less visible to his—or her—enemies. After all, the point was to protect the heir, not to have him fight battles. The guard returned bearing lighter, and softer, undergarments to cushion the armor.

"Thank you, Uncle. I am in your debt."

"Mine! Hardly. That's the least I can do. You show up with an army in my time of need. That will not be forgotten."

His eyes darkened with the shadows of the memory of insults and slights over the years from the Hildes of Taivasta that he overlooked so as not to plunge into an unnecessary war. Greylin remembered the words of the innkeeper at the Tumbling Turtle. Many people must wonder if the King of Castabal would one day say "Enough!" and ride north to extract vengeance.

"You have shown great forbearance over the years, Uncle. I thank you for that. There would be many who live now who would have died otherwise."

He looked at her in startled surprise, "Yes, exactly. I wish to go with you, but I would have to overrule my family, my advisors, and my guards. Staying behind does not please me. Will I let my niece fight for me?"

"I did not see you in my visions, so do not fret on that account," she assured him. "If we were to fail, you will have your hands full here, but I do not think we will."

Greylin looked over at Hollinghast and D'Arcannon who were beaming with approval. They, in turn, thanked the king for his generosity. They, too, did not want her to go to the east at all. They wanted her to stay in Torilinna Castle and be protected by ranks of guards, but they knew, as did she, the visions required her to be there. In each path, where she was not there, swarms of Jonjishalan crawled over the land without ceasing.

They agreed to leave in two hours.

The land they traveled was lush, water flowed everywhere, in pools, canals, streams, waterfalls, and springs. Wherever there was water, plants flourished. It was a land burgeoning with abundance. Greylin could not imagine what it would look like if the Jonji crawled over it.

They arrived safely at the garrison of Tower Adelia the next day. There were three main garrisons with lookout points and signal fire towers, the other two were Tower Grace in the south and Tower Claire in the center. Adelia was the furthest north where the Tammerlin Strait was the narrowest. It was thought that they would cross there first.

There were rock formations to the north of the camp. Red rocks that rose up and formed peaks, hollows, and bridges. Greylin was fascinated by them, she had seen swirling reds one time when she wore the crown, but it seemed meaningless. Now that vision made sense.

They reported to Commander Rayne Salazar who sorted out where they should position their camp. He was a tall man, graying, who looked perpetually worried. They assured him that they had brought fresh provisions from Rimmon. He was noticeably relieved because he hadn't planned on accommodating another five hundred plus fighting men. They set up camp and waited. Greylin wondered if she should use the crown to see if she could find out with greater certainty when an attack would come. *I could,* she thought, *but I already know. It will be soon.*

Rilah stayed back in Rimmon with Rilann. They were catching up on many things, and Rilann would not leave the king's side in a time of danger. Rilah was not a fighter and Greylin asked that she stay safely behind but then regretted her decision when she needed help with the armor; it wasn't something she could manage on her own.

After changing in her tent to the soft inner wear to protect her body from the metal, she called Finn in and handed him the armor. He would have to help in lieu of Rilah. They looked at it and tried to figure out what came first. They tried laying it out on her cot to see how all the pieces went together. When they got to the codpiece they just fell apart laughing.

"I can't wear that!" Greylin exclaimed.

"Well, you can't skip it either!" Finn replied. "You know, it would be a chink in the armor and an arrow could get through."

"I don't think the Jonjishalan have arrows, but that would be a terrible way to die!"

That sent them into a gale of giggles. Eventually, they gave up trying to figure all the pieces out, and Finn went to find D'Arcannon.

"We need some help," Greylin said as he entered the tent.

"So Finn tells me," he replied without laughing. *Bless him,* she thought.

"You have to start at the bottom and work your way up. Everything overlaps. Sabatons first," he indicated.

"What?"

"The shoes."

"Oh."

They got the shoes on her. She walked around a bit. They were fine. Not too big as she thought they would be when she looked at them. Next came the greaves on her shins. They had a lot of play for width and that went okay. And then the cod piece. Finn and Greylin started laughing again, and D'Arcannon had to leave the tent for a moment saying, "Let me know when that's on."

She assumed he didn't want to embarrass her. That made the giggling uncontrollable. She managed it a while later and Finn called him back in. He had that half-smile on his face. On up through the cuirass, bracers, pauldrons, and gauntlets and except for the helmet, she was done.

"How do you feel?" D'Arcannon asked.

"I'm afraid to move. I've become all stiff."

"It's not that bad, really. You need to walk around to get used to it. Let's go practice."

"What?"

"Best way to get used to it. Where's your sword?"

Finn handed it to her, and they went out to find a wide, flat space. Every time she moved, she clanked. The armor wasn't that heavy, only 30 or 40 pounds and distributed nicely. It fit well, too; she just couldn't get used to the noise she made.

Of course, they attracted an audience. *When don't I?* she thought. D'Arcannon led her through the exercises, slowly at first then faster, and she started getting used to the fact that she could move around easily despite the noise. Soon she got into it and they really started sparring. They were going at it fiercely when he finally signaled to stop.

"Better?" he asked.

"Much. Thank you. That is what I needed. You always know, of course. What about the helmet though?"

"That's next. I wanted you to get past being afraid to move. Finn?"

He ran back into the tent and got the helmet.

"Okay, put that on, and let's go through it one more time."

She put the helmet on and immediately felt closed in. She hated the fact that her side vision was blocked off.

"It makes you focus on what's in front of you," D'Arcannon said as he moved around her, slowly increasing the speed of his attacks. "That's a little scary at first, but remember, you have protection from all sides. If someone attacks you from the side, they're not going to hurt you. You can then turn your attention to them if need be. Don't worry about whether you can see it, or him, or not. Your horse will be able to see and move accordingly. Well, he should. I'm not sure about what Roki will do. He might be better at it than most, or worse. The thing is, stay out of the fray if you can. I know you have to be here. I don't like it one bit, but that's the way it is. But no risks, please!"

Greylin nodded and took the helmet off. The men sent up a cheer. She smiled and waved at them. She hoped they had a little more faith in her now that they had seen her fight with a paladin.

The cheer was cut off as the fire signal was lit on Tower Adelia. The flames rose high and sent off black daytime smoke so that the other towers could relay the message. Horns sounded and the battle was on.

Chapter 24

FIRST ATTACK

*"Never desire to hurt another, but if you must kill to
survive, do it quickly and blame yourself not."*

- LAMENT OF THE MAZARINES

Greylin strained to see across the straight but the
Jonjishalan were too far out and only visible from the
tower. She mounted Roki and waited. She knew they
weren't going to let her any closer to the shore. Finn had
been sent to the back with the wagons and fresh horses. He
wasn't happy about it. He was strong and resourceful, but
he was no trained fighter. If Tower Adelia fell, he was
charged with returning to Rimmon and alerting them.
Hollinghast was poised on the lower cliffs with the
Lumerians, and she could hear the sounds of kanteles and
kantelyres mixed with a choir of men's voices as they
prepared spells together. D'Arcannon and his men formed
a wall of man and horse at the edge of the water.

She heard men yelling, "Here they come!" and
"They're swimming the strait," and thought she could hear
the "jonji" sound. It was so mindless. Like the sounds
crickets make in the late summer. "jonji, jonji, jonji' but
not as high pitched. It was more like obnoxious chewing.

The sea was churning, and a cold chill rose from her
stomach to her chest. She began to repeat the litany before
battle: *"I stand as one with ELIEL, between the EL Within
and the EL Without, the Above and Below, between the
Darkness and the Light. Nothing can hurt me. ELIEL
protects me, ELIEL defends me, ELIEL preserves my
spirit. Here in the Now, there is no Place where EL is not.
EL surrounds me, EL protects me, EL sustains me. I shall*

not fear, I shall not despair. I AM EL. I am Safe. I am Eternal. Only Love will Prevail. She added, *Even if I were to fall in battle, I am still in the Grace of ELIEL and live forevermore."*

Greylin began to relax as she repeated the comforting words of faith. She was well in the back and still could not see enough to suit her. She was growing impatient and looked around for a vantage point. There on the left in the red hills she could see an out-of-the-way path that led up to a ledge where she might be able to get high enough to see what was going on. To her surprise no one challenged her. Everyone's attention was at the front, not along the back. She rode up a low rise to the first set of hills. She could see that they were intersected with many paths, probably from wildlife or wandering humans posted at Adelia. She continued to climb and was finally able to see where the creatures were swimming across the strait.

Thousands of bodies were making their way across. They chanted as they swam. There was something so mindless about them that it made her shiver. She edged Roki up across a rock bridge between two hills and watched in growing horror. As the Jonji reached the shore, some of them stood up on two legs and grappled with their top four arms. Once the fighting began, they stopped chanting "jonji" and started saying "shalan". The continuous "shush" was unnerving combined with the repetitive "j" sound from the ones in the rear.

On their back legs, the Jonji were taller than most of the men, so having troops on horses was essential. Other Jonji crawled on four legs, some on all six, and they just seemed to keep going unless they were stopped. *They're like giant, fleshy ants,* she thought. Various shades of sparse, dingy brown hair covered their paler skin, their pinched waists were caked with dirt that had not loosened even though they swam the entire strait. They had claws with long, pincer-type talons on the first two digits of their front appendages. As they attacked, they grabbed with their front arms and ripped live flesh with their lip-less mouths and gnashing teeth that clamped and held. They bit anywhere on the body, anywhere they could reach, and overcame their foes by sheer numbers and mindless persistence. Some of the Brigade and Castabalian soldiers were unintentionally wearing the heads of some of the creatures who stayed attached by their mouths to pieces of armor or chainmail. One soldier even wore one whose head was biting another Jonji head, both attached to his armor behind him. There was no time to hack them off, and they would not let go even in death.

The most terrifying thing was that when either a soldier or one of the Jonji was injured, the creatures ate a few quick mouthfuls and then carried the body along. It didn't matter if the body was human or Jonji! Those that were burdened with such a body were easily killed, thus saving many a soldier who might have met a more horrible fate later in the day.

Greylin could see D'Arcannon cutting swaths in the ranks below. She was relieved to see that he was using both sword and dagger and that his complex rules of engagement didn't include having to use hand-to-hand combat with the creatures. He had already set a rhythm, chopping off their forearms with his sword and then dispatching them in heart or neck with his dagger. Sprays of dirty yellow blood flew through the air with each strike, blending with the red of humans. It formed a ghastly orange mist that nearly obscured them. A rising pile of bodies was being hurriedly dragged away to give the warriors rooms to fight.

Hollinghast was blasting the beasts, but it wasn't deterring them. The smell of burning hair and flesh hung in the air. Still, on and on they came. The Golden Brigade was staying together and fighting well; the Castabal army, too, but the Jonji seemed to be winning with sheer numbers. She could still see them coming far out in the strait.

Greylin pulled her sword. She remembered this scene below from one of the visions when she wore the crown. The red rocks, her arm dark (now she knew the red streaks were the rocks behind her and her arm dark because of the black armor), her sword raised high. Hollinghast caught sight of her out of the corner of his eye. He must have seen the same vision and remembered it too. He transferred the lightning so that it looked as though it came out of the tip of Greylin's sword. The sword, in turn, pulled lightning from the sky.

After the first few shocks hit them, the Jonji looked up. This was strangely out of character. It stopped the flow of the advance, and the "shalan" chant paused for a breathless moment. Hollinghast blasted them again, and with the help of the other mages, managed to make it into a continuous stream. The creatures began to back away in fear. Greylin wasn't sure what they were afraid of, but it was working so they kept it up.

What she could not see was the picture they were creating. Here was a black figure on a Leopard Horse on a high arched rock bridge shooting lightning at them. There was something sinister and otherworldly in that scene that scared them on a deep instinctive level. They began retreating back over the advancing ranks. Clouds rolled in and the scene darkened. The "shalan" noises had stopped. There was only the "jonji" chant now as they turned and swam back the way they came.

Once Hollinghast and Greylin were sure the Jonjishalan were retreating, they ended their efforts and returned to camp. Shortly after arriving at her tent, Hollinghast entered.

"That was close," he said.

"It's why we had to be here," Greylin answered.

"They'll be back."

"I know. I have to use the Crown again. We can't afford to lose. I don't know what they were planning with the bodies, but I can't help thinking that a force that size needs a lot of food."

They exchanged grim looks.

Chapter 25

BEST LAID PLANS

*No plan is perfect but having no plan
at all is a disaster.*

- Letters of Queen Hiilda

The soldiers lined the shore and watched the Jonjishalan swim back across the strait. *It was so far to swim! How strong were they?* When the ones returning encountered one swimming towards them the people on shore tried to understand what was communicated but couldn't quite grasp it. Sometimes one would just keep swimming towards the shore anyway, but eventually, the sheer number of retreating Jonji seemed to convince the creatures to turn. Or that's what they guessed.

Finally, the weary soldiers were able to return to camp for hearty meals prepared by the cooks next to the wagons. The bodies of some of the soldiers had been dragged back with the retreating swimmers. It didn't seem possible that they could swim all the way back with them. The loss of their men, and the fact that their bodies would never be recovered was disturbing, but the thought of what might be done with them if they were not dead was horrifying.

Greylin walked through the ranks, looking for men who had lost friends. She comforted them and praised them for their efforts, thanking them for helping to prevent a worse invasion. She told them the enemy would be back. The war wasn't over, but they had held them for now.

She saved her tears for the privacy of her tent. Men she had sat with night after night, men she sang with, men she had come to know, were hurt or missing because of their loyalty to her. Some of the youngest were missing. And it was not yet over.

Green smoke was pouring from watchtower Adelia above them to notify the other towers that the enemy had retreated. There had been no indication that there was an attack at the other two sites. There were more troops there, and whether those troops should be pulled away to reinforce Camp Adelia was the question of the moment.

Greylin sought out Hollinghast and asked him and Finn to come to her tent. She needed to place the Elder Crown on her head once more and find the right course to take. D'Arcannon was tending to his armor, his horse, and his weapons, so she left him to it. She wondered how many he had killed. The bodies piled up and were taken away again and again. It would be safe to say he may have killed over a hundred by himself.

Greylin sat on a camp stool with Finn on one side and Hollinghast behind her. He placed the crown on her head and she slammed backward against the tall mage as the visions kicked in, but he was prepared for it and braced her. *Click, click, click,* the doors opened this way and that. She tried to focus on their victory, right here and now, and slow the rush of possibilities. She decided to form words— a question—clear and simple. *When will the Jonjishalan attack again?* She immediately flew down a corridor— they were swimming in the same impossibly great numbers. It was morning, early light. But what day? What day?

She saw herself getting up from the camp stool she sat in, rapidly going through her day and retiring for the night. Then the whole next day and night. It was disconcerting to see herself doing things she hadn't yet done. Another day and night and then an early morning advance. *So, not tomorrow, or the next but the one after that. Good. That will give us time to plan...but what about the other towers?* The Jonjishalan swam across the strait at its narrowest, but as their numbers increased and they met with resistance, some were choosing to swim to the south. Rocky cliffs along the water's edge rose straight up and deterred them from coming ashore, but they still tried it, grasping at every ridge in the sheer rocks until they inevitably fell, their bodies lying broken upon the rocks below. Some swam all the way to the south and made it to the next landing at Camp Grace.

She ripped the crown off and told Hollinghast what she had seen. The three of them went directly to Commander Salazar. Someone needed to warn Grace Tower but there was no smoke pattern to explain so complicated a message. Someone would have to go, but they needed every fighting man at Adelia because they would still face the brunt of the attack.

"Finn can do it!" Greylin.

"And I have my own horse," Finn added. One had been purchased for him in Sessirra for him and he was quite proud of it. "But I don't know the way."

"There is a clear road. Just follow this one south," Salazar replied.

Greylin was pleased, Finn would feel useful yet safely away from the fighting.

It was a day's ride, no more, from one tower to another. They would have more than enough time to prepare if he left immediately. Commander Salazar wrote out a report and handed it to Finn in a metal container.

"Goodbye, Finn," Greylin said hugging him. "Take care and stay out of trouble."

"I will. Running or swimming, I'm faster than you."

She laughed. "That's true, though I hate to admit it. You can row pretty good, too."

They laughed again, remembering their trip to rescue Hollinghast and D'Arcannon on a false trail across the Pearladen Bay. Finn had handed her the oars without realizing that she had no idea how to row. She had learned in a hurry—probably the fastest lesson ever.

Finn waved as he trotted off. Greylin felt a pang of concern, but he didn't need her to watch over him.

They returned to Salazar and began to talk strategy. He had a map spread out on a table outside his tent and discussed how the attack might come. The hills on the north concentrated the attack to the center of the shoreline of the camp and to the south. If they could force them into a narrower area, they'd have a better chance of controlling the advance. They needed to block them from turning south.

Salazar suggested, "We could line up the wagons and try to channel them into a narrow area, though it would be easy for them to crawl underneath."

"How about a pit?" Greylin suggested. "The dirt can be piled up on the sides to make it deeper. Position some men up above on either side of the pit with crossbows, and they can pick off any that might crawl out over the others. We have just enough time."

Commander Salazar looked at her in surprise. "That might work," he said, running his thumb along his chin.

"There's one flaw in the plan though." Salazar pointed out. "There's no reason why the ones veering south can't just come up behind the lines shooting across the pit. They'll be behind the lines and squeeze us in the middle."

"They won't," Greylin replied. "Because I'll be there. I know where the break point is—where they change direction. I've seen it. I can position myself where they would veer off and force them back toward the center."

"I don't like the sounds of that—that places you in danger," Salazar said.

"Not with Hollinghast behind me," she looked up at him and smiled. "We already know the lightning effect shooting from my sword repels or terrifies them. We will take advantage of that."

"I won't let anything happen to her. We have just enough time to dig that trench if we start right away. I can help with the singing," Hollinghast offered.

"That would be most appreciated, Master Mage." The work would go faster and the walls would hold better if magic strengthened the men as they worked and the walls as they went up.

Work details began to dig, and Hollinghast and a few of the other Lumerians began to sing. After his first song which he sang alone and was an invocation to ELIEL, they began a rhythmic working song that the men soon picked up. They sang in cadence and call-back, shoveled, and patted the sandy walls under the wagons for most of the day before they struck water about thirty hands down and called a halt to the project. The Commander pronounced it deep enough, however, and a cheer went up. The mages finished off reinforcing the walls of the pit with a few complicated songs and the job was done. The men were heartened.

Sometimes doing something that even looks like it might work can change things around, Greylin thought. *It restores faith.*

Chapter 26

SECOND ATTACK

*"For the beasts gathered as locusts and joined with
the blasphemer to devour the whole of the earth."*

-REVELATIONS BY TIMON THE HERMIT

That night they slept fitfully. Greylin went over and
over the plan in her mind but resisted putting on the Crown
to see if it would work. She chastised herself for not
wanting to do it but still didn't want to go through the
dizzying experience. And she thought, *maybe I don't want
to see if it will fail because so much has been invested in
it.* She wondered how Finn was making out and hoped he
had made it to Garrison Grace and that they were prepared.

Finally, shortly before dawn, she crept over to the
Crown and took it back to bed with her. She reasoned that
if she was lying down, she couldn't fall over. *How can I
risk everyone's lives without being sure of what I'm doing?
Even if it makes me look like a fool.*

She placed the Crown on her head and tried to focus
on the coming battle. The Crown would not cooperate.
Perhaps she had worried too much and the Crown was
done with her concerns? But no, there was a strange city
with streets that did not look like Sessirra. She soared
above and looked right and left to see if the ocean was
nearby—it wasn't—and it wasn't by Castabal either
because it just wasn't watery enough, and she had a good
idea what it would look like from above.

Madhia perhaps, or even New Saar? She couldn't see
anything that told her one way or another. She tried to
jump ahead a little and there was a sea of angry faces

passing close, talking and shouting, but she couldn't hear what they were saying.

She slipped the Crown off her head and tried to sort out what it had told her. She must have drifted off for the next thing she knew, the sun was shining, horses were moving around, stamping and snorting, and men were shouting as they went about setting up for the day. She stepped out of her tent and saw Hollinghast and D'Arcannon sitting by the campfire sharing tea. Her eyes filled with tears. She had grown so fond of them, and so fond of being on the road with them. The simple scene of the two of them sitting by the campfire was threatened by so many things. She wouldn't allow herself to think of either of them falling in the coming battle, but it could happen, and even if it didn't, once she returned to New Saar—if she survived—her camping days would be over.

She squeezed the tears from her eyes and sent up a silent prayer to ELIEL to sustain them in the flow of life today and forgive them for the slaughter that was to come. She was acting a lot more confident on the outside than she was feeling on the inside.

She sat down with them as she had every day for the past few months but had barely finished a mug of tea before the alarm horns sounded. D'Arcannon and Greylin saluted each other, and then she thought, *the heck with it,* and gave him a hug. He would be holding the line in the center, and she feared for the onslaught he would have to endure. He was surprised but hugged her back warmly, then sternly cautioned her to be careful. *Were those tears in his eyes? Did Paladins cry?*

Hollinghast and Greylin then looked at each other and nodded. It was time. She mounted—she would be on Roki—but Hollinghast had sent Merelda to the rearmost position and safety. The white mare didn't like it one bit, but he was not going to risk her, she was no warhorse. He had been singing most of the night, storing up magic in his songs for the day. Greylin worried about him not getting any rest. *How long could he keep going like this?*

They all rushed to their positions. They could see the sea churning once again as the Jonjishalan approached. She trembled. There were so many! She felt fear run through her body like cold water. Roki snorted as if to tell her to *stop it*. He had no fear and he wasn't going to allow her any. Greylin took heart. Hollinghast positioned himself on her left, staff in hand, with two other mages to help. One behind and one to her right.

The Jonji were shortly upon them. The plan was working. Jonji swarmed onto the shore and crowded into the channel they had made for them, blocked by hills and cliffs on the creatures' right and left, they were forced to the pit where they balked. The ones behind kept pushing, and soon the forerunners were toppling in. She couldn't help feeling both surprise and relief.

Some tried to climb up the sides by standing on others and were easily killed by the crossbowmen positioned above. Those coming Greylin's way veered away to the north when they neared her and Hollinghast. As unnerving as it was to see them approach, she was able to observe them and some part of her coldly analyzed the situation.

She noticed that they were looking at Roki, not her, or even Hollinghast. It was Roki who filled them with terror. It was a bit funny: *who do I think I am that they would be afraid of me? They are only afraid of my horse!* She thought about it some more and it began to make sense. The people of Allanda knew almost nothing about where and how the Jonjishalan lived. No one knew what kinds of spotted creatures surrounded them. If there were Snow Leopards there, maybe other spotted creatures— *snakes?*—and even Leopard Horses like Roki who hated them, then their fear would be for all spotted things! Greylin thanked ELIEL for bringing such a magical horse to her in this time of need.

Hollinghast was holding back his "lightning" attacks. She could understand why, they had no idea if they would be needed more later in the day. So far, the plan was working but it was limited in how many could be handled.

Greylin wondered how they were doing in the back where most of them were being funneled. It seemed like there was a lot going on, clanking, shouting, the raspy wails of the Jonji as they fell, and the more heartbreaking cries of men. She could hear D'Arcannon's horse screaming in anger; and she turned to catch a glimpse of the huge black pounding the Jonji with his hooves and ripping them with his teeth. She thought he must be loving it; he finally got to express all that bottled up hostility.

All seemed to go as planned for the first few hours but as the day wore on, the onslaught became so relentless that it was wearying and disturbing. *How many were there?* They could see no end in sight, and far out to sea the water still churned.

The chant of "jonji" and "shalan" wore on their nerves. As time went on the numbers became heavier, and it became harder and harder to repel them all. The pit below the wagons had filled up, so that now when the creatures were funneled in, they simply climbed over the bodies below. The crossbowmen were running out of bolts and could not recover them from the bodies.

Hollinghast was starting to blast the ones veering toward them in greater numbers. Now he and Greylin were being pushed back from the shore, the ones swimming behind were pushing the others into them and they weren't turning away as quickly from Roki. She had no choice but to fight them, and the sword sang with fury.

The ones they killed were piled high around them. Greylin had to back up twice, a few feet more and she would be in the line of a stray shot from the crossbows aimed from the red rocks above the wagons on the north side.

The plan was good, but it could fail due to sheer numbers. They just kept coming! She was tiring and knew everyone else was as well. The sword seemed to have a will of its own, though, and her arm swung with deadly accuracy in spite of her fatigue.

The sun was beginning to descend behind her, and she worried about how the soldiers would manage during the night if the attack continued. The strait was dark from clouds building in the east, and she could not see if the creatures were still swimming toward them that far away.

The press of attackers increased oppressively in front of her. There were so many they crowded each other which prevented their ability to avoid Roki. It was sickening. The Jonji had no weapons, so it was not so much a fight as a struggling slaughter.

The creatures' long arms posed the greatest danger. She was forced to cut those off before being able to deliver a mortal strike. She would not have known where to strike, but the Sword Argente aimed true and fast, and bodies began to pile higher around her. She was holding her own and Hollinghast was cutting swaths with lightshock spells; but she could not back up, she could not go forward, and she was steeling herself against panic. A searing pain of fatigue started from her shoulder and ran down to her wrist. She gritted her teeth against the pain and vowed to keep going though she might die trying.

She was dimly aware of a thunderous sound and thought that the darkening clouds had turned into a storm. Lightning flashed from the rear in the growing darkness. The thunder grew louder in a steady rumble. A shout went up and she feared the troops behind her were being overrun. But—no, it was cheering!

A host of paladins, warriors, mages, and singers rode furiously past her and attacked the Jonji along the front lines. She had forgotten about the other Mazarines and Lumerians who had been alerted! She cheered and whooped with the rest of the tired warriors retreating to the back to make way for the newcomers who were fresh and strong.

Chapter 27

AFTERMATH

"We are deathless says the soul;
we are broken says the heart."

-A TRAGEDY IN THREE ACTS
BY THE BARD OF MADHIA

The reinforcements fought steadily for three hours and then abruptly, there were no more Jonji swimming the strait. Greylin had lost any sense of how many Jonji headed south. They had sustained hour after hour of battle, and there was no way to see how many were still in the water veering to the south while she was hacking away at the ones in front of her. Green smoke went up from the tower signaling victory and cheers erupted at the sight.

They began to take stock of their losses. Greylin found D'Arcannon sitting by a fire a little way across the camp. He looked more exhausted than Greylin had ever seen him. He had been positioned dead center at the end point where the Jonji were channeled and had taken the brunt of the attack. He fought for hours and without faltering. She walked over and sat down beside him.

"You are well? You have no injuries?" she asked, feeling strange because he was usually asking her those questions.

"A couple broken fingers, cuts, and bruises, but I am whole in body. I cannot say the same for Bane," he said softly.

Greylin's throat tightened in fear, "Oh no! What?"

"He is injured, badly. He is barely alive."

Bane was such a fierce fighter, a magnificent horse that Greylin could not imagine ever being defeated. Reist's sorrow was nearly palpable. Hollinghast had told her that Bane was D'Arcannon's second horse. His first, Thunder, was a devastating loss for him. Even Hollinghast didn't know all the details and D'Arcannon said little, only that it was a freak shot from a robber with a crossbow. That grief must have still been upon him. And now this. To lose one was tragedy enough, but if he were to lose two!

"Can I get you anything to drink or eat?" Greylin asked quietly.

"No, no. I had something a while ago. The healers insisted."

Greylin thought of all the losses she had sustained in her past lives; the sorrow and grief would be overwhelming if people were born remembering it. The world is a place of breathtaking beauty, but it is also harsh, cruel, and often unfair. Anyone, looking around would think such beauty must indicate a blissful life, but no one reaches the end of it without their hearts being broken.

Most young people, like her, feel they are invincible because they have forgotten their grief, and they come into the world trailing the peace and glory of the eternal otherworld, but she remembered. It would come to everyone sooner or later. It is what they do then that makes all the difference.

"What happened?" she asked.

"They swarmed us and even though he had armor, the monsters would bite anything they could reach. They would grab with those pincers and hang on. They went at his legs and at some point, he simply had no ground to stand on because there were so many bodies in the way. He stumbled, and I was being attacked, from behind. He fell one way and I went another. I had no room to turn and save him and when next I was able to look; he was nowhere in sight. We did not find him until the Jonjishalan dead had all been cleared." He smiled grimly, "He still had the arm of one of them between his teeth."

They continued to sit without speaking. She could not help herself—she put her arm around him, and they sat in silence for a few moments until Roki came up behind and nudged her with his nose. She thought *not now* at him, but he stamped his foot. She grimaced in irritation then got the impression that he was looking for Bane.

"Where is he now?" she asked.

He motioned toward the healers' tent. "Over there, they minister to the men first, the horses come later. They did give him something for pain and then kicked me out because they said I was in the way."

"I'm going to check on him," she said and rose to her feet. D'Arcannon started to say something, then just nodded. They might let her in, she was a little bit of a thing compared to him.

Greylin and Roki slipped through the camp and peered into the healers' tents. It was a depressing sight, and she realized she should have come earlier to give comfort where she could. She saw no horses though and continued walking to the back. Finally, in a field with a few tent coverings rigged up to shield the patients from the sun were the horses. Roki led the way; he must have sensed where Bane would be. The big black was lying on the ground, breathing in raspy breaths. She sat down next to him and stroked his huge neck. Roki snuffled around him from nose to tail. He seemed to be evaluating the big horse's condition. Then he did an odd thing. He laid down next to Bane and placed his neck and head over the black's big body and began to make a bizarre huffing and groaning sound.

Was he crying? she wondered. It was a continuous sound that went up and down in scale. He also was trembling and seemed to be stuck to Bane and unable to move. Greylin had no idea what to do. *Should she separate them? Was Roki hurt? Should they leave them alone?* The weird sound attracted some of the healers who gathered around and whispered to each other, then one said, "Get Sven" and a younger orderly took off.

The crooning continued until she heard a voice behind her say, "Oh good bones, it is the Fell Healing. Thank ELIEL for this help," then the man, the one named Sven, who had spoken got down on his knees and stroked Bane's head. "He will live now. The Fell Healing heals all."

Greylin looked at him, eyes wide, "What is that?"

"This pony is wit' you? I heard about that but wasn't sure to believe it."

"Yes, yes, this is Roki. I think I am his not the other way around."

Sven laughed, "Aye, that's what they say."

Roki chose that moment to rise and chew on some grass like nothing had happened.

"Come here, Sven has better than that for you," he motioned to Roki who followed him docilely.

Greylin jumped up realizing that she was being left behind. She followed them both until they reached a supply tent and Sven dished out some sweetened oats which Roki scarfed down as though he hadn't eaten in days. Sven looked at her, "the healing takes a lot out of them. They need to replenish."

"How do you know all this?" she asked.

"Oh, ah, erm, Sven knows. Seen many years, many horses. Yah. Sven heals. Only sees one Fell Horse but Sven saw the healing. No one believes Sven. Now they do. Sven very grateful."

Roki finished the oats, blew and shook his head. Greylin was fascinated by the way Sven referred to himself.

"We have some others, badly wounded. Ask him if he would help; Sven has lots more oats," he shook the bucket enticingly.

Greylin did her best to construct a similar scene to what she had just witnessed. Roki nodded his head up and down and nosed the oat bucket.

Sven laughed, "Goot then, follow Sven."

"Just waltz right off," Greylin murmured to herself. She had never seen the horse behave like that before. Sven must have some powerful horse magic.

She returned to Bane and was thrilled to see he had rolled up. He wasn't on his feet yet, but he looked like a different horse already. She squatted down next to him, "I'm going to get Reist, I'll be right back."

She trotted back to where she had left D'Arcannon. His eyes were closed, and his shoulders slumped. Three of his fingers were in splints. He must be utterly exhausted. Let's hope this news will let him rest. She touched his shoulder gently, "Reist, come with me."

He looked up at her blearily but rose as she requested. She led him to Bane, and he brightened like a child with a present. "Bane! You're okay!"

They reacquainted for a few moments and then D'Arcannon looked saddened again. Greylin moved closer.

"Aye, the damage to the legs," a green-robed healer was telling him. "His fighting days are over. He is good for stud still and has deserved a rest, but no more fightin'."

Bane looked ashamed, as though he had somehow failed. D'Arcannon picked up on that immediately. He sat on the ground and hugged that great neck, speaking quietly to him until Bane's eyes closed in relieved comfort. Greylin stepped away, eyes swimming, and returned to camp.

A few hours later Greylin and D'Arcannon were sharing a meal when a remarkable thing happened. A large—amazingly sleek—Midnight Friesian walked slowly up to the fire across from D'Arcannon and waited. Greylin looked at D'Arcannon—he wouldn't look at the horse—and she could feel his stubborn resistance. *Oh,* she thought, *it's too soon.*

The horse continued to wait patiently, looking at D'Arcannon, then blew once in the way horses do and dipped his head. Greylin was openly staring. She couldn't believe what a beauty he was, his coat shone like flaked obsidian in the firelight. He was even bigger than Bane, heavily muscled, so dark a shade of black that the light shone dark blue where it touched him. More impressive than that were his eyes! They were full of intelligence and wisdom.

D'Arcannon glanced up but dropped his eyes again. There was a lot going on that no one else could fully be part of. The horse blew and stamped, then whinnied gently. D'Arcannon finally looked up at him. The wave of love and understanding that beamed from the horse was so strong that some of it spilled over onto Greylin, and her eyes watered. She was sure that D'Arcannon was radiating a deep, heartbreaking pain, but also knew the horse was absorbing it without flinching.

Finally, their eyes locked, and a long, silent conversation took place. Both horse and man knew that lives were at stake, not the least would be their own. The agreement had to be between them, that each in their turn was willing to suffer that hurt again. The emotions were so raw, Greylin had to look away.

Finally, D'Arcannon got up and man and horse walked off behind the healers' wagons. *They will see Bane,* she thought, *and get his blessing.*

Chapter 28

FAREWELLS

*"For every beginning there is an ending,
and looking back, the beginning becomes
sweeter and the ending more bitter."*

- THE DIARY OF LADY RILAH OF THE ISLAND

The next day, Greylin went in search of Hollinghast who she found resting in a hammock by his tent. The Viridian Healers had insisted on him doing nothing, and after a battle, no one had more clout than the Healers. The mages were dangerously low on life force, having used so much to sing before and throughout the battle, that they needed to stop and renew. The Singers who had just arrived could take over in case of any sightings of Jonjishalan.

"What exactly happened between Reist and that new horse?" she asked, and then wondered when she had started calling him "Reist".

"The horse has chosen him. A paladin's horse picks him, not the other way around. Sadly, whenever the Mazarines go out to a battle like this, they bring extra horses—or I should say, some horses choose to go. They know that there will be casualties.

"The horse does the choosing, but the rider has to allow it. Sometimes they can't, either because they aren't willing to risk it again, or because they've been injured and cannot honor the horse in combat. This happened to the Kevic twins in New Saar. Both were injured and did not take new mounts because they were found too late for the Healers to completely restore them to their fighting strength. One because of his arm, the other because of his leg. They are Canons now in the cathedral instead. Still serving but not as warriors, and without the great Friesians. You might meet them when we get to New Saar.

"It is nothing to make light of by any means. I don't know how I'd handle it if I lost Merelda in battle, or in some other, terrible way. That's why I won't take her. She's angry with me because of that. She'll be cold toward me for the next few days. Maybe I should bring her in here so she can start now—and maybe get it over with sooner. Could you fetch her for me? If the Healers see me out and about, they'll skin me alive, and then I'd have to put up with them even longer."

Greylin laughed and stood up, "One more thing," she paused. "What about when the rider is lost but the horse survives?"

"Then the horse is free to choose again or retire. That's where the other horses come from."

She looked at him in puzzlement.

"The foals," he said drily. "In the mountains they roam freely."

"Oh," she laughed. "I never thought about that. Where are they raised?"

"Along the foothills of the Tyhja Mountains. They say that's where they were first found."

"I see," she looked down at her feet thoughtfully. "I'll be right back," she said and left the tent.

I'd sure like to see those hills, and the horses running below them, she mused. As soon as she thought it, she got a brief flash of memory: bright green rolling hills, white-capped mountains in the distance, and the sound of thundering hooves as a herd of black horses swept over a rise. Their manes and tails were flying in the wind and they were achingly beautiful...

Apparently, she had been there once, sometime. It was like a glimpse of heaven. *That's what we fight for,* a voice inside her head said. *Where did that voice come from? Who's we?* She asked. But there was no answer. She shook herself into the here and now and walked back to find Merelda.

Castillo's men continued to send up green smoke from Tower Adelia to indicate victory. She found Merelda and gathered the mare's halter in her hand to lead her back. Tower Claire was sending up black smoke! The enemy had been sighted, perhaps even engaged. She hoped Finn had given them enough warning, so they were prepared.

The Mazarines were already mounted, except for D'Arcannon whose vows kept him to Greylin's side, and all but one healer wagon was preparing to depart. The Golden Brigade would stay behind in case another wave of Jonji hit Camp Adelia —they also refused to leave Greylin—but the others would head to Camp Grace to reinforce them.

They thundered off south, and Greylin led Merelda to Hollinghast's tent. The mare was happy to see her, but as he had anticipated, she was angry and refused to look at him when she returned. She even stood with her back end facing him!

The Lumerians stayed until Salazar's men finished building a pyre for the dead. Horses and men alike were laid together and their names were read aloud. If there had been only one or two, they would have placed them in a boat and sent them out to sea, setting it on fire far from shore. When there were many—so many!—as there were today, a small boat would be sent out symbolically, carrying their names on slips of parchment with blessings, prayers, flowers, tokens, and mementos. The strongest swimmers took the boat out, in this case one made from one of the wagons, far enough offshore so that it would not be swept back. Once they returned, many of the mages gathered and began to sing. Hollinghast and a few others were excluded, still deemed too spent to participate, but the rest donned their whitest robes and the group of them seemed to glow.

As they sang, small flames appeared and danced along the top of the pyre and along the edge of the boat, building in size and heat as the singing grew in volume. The song was sad and heart-wrenching. How they managed to continue singing without crying was a wonder because everyone who wasn't singing was tearful.

As the flames soared upwards the song changed from one of unbearable sadness to one that filled the heart with courage and the willingness to sacrifice oneself for all that is good and pure in the world, for beauty's sake, for the sake of the innocent. It was the same song, yet now it strengthened their resolve.

Greylin was standing next to D'Arcannon and his new horse stood on his left; Roki standing at her right, for all the horses were in attendance as well. She had one arm on Roki, and could not help herself; she placed her left on D'Arcannon's arm. To her surprise he raised that mighty arm and placed it around her shoulders. She fit her arm around his waist and leaned into him. *My champion,* she thought, and then she heard that other voice in her head say, *forevermore.*

Chapter 29

LEAVING ADELIA

"Losing a loved one fills one with grief, but at least it is finished for better or ill; not knowing the fate of a loved one eats steadily at the heart with an endless sorrow."

- *THE JONJI WARS* BY ST. ANSELM THE VIRIDIAN

Two days later, all but the soldiers permanently stationed at Camp Adelia were packing up to leave. Greylin had determined that there would be no more attacks after wearing the Elder Crown. She and the Golden Brigade, as well as a cohort of the remaining Lumerians and Mazarines, headed south to Camp Grace. Greylin's attention was on finding Finn as much as securing Grace. Finn probably stayed for the battle. She hoped he didn't get hurt. They sent him to keep him out of danger, not into it.

Before they left, Tower Grace sent up green smoke indicating victory, so she asked the Brigade to meet her in Rimmon. She wanted to move fast, and they would have slowed them down. There was no reason to push them either. They deserved rest and healing, but she was met with stubborn protests and a compromise was reached where an escort of six followed her led by Captain Redmond. She had lost thirty men, all told. Her heart grieved for them.

D'Arcannon was riding his new mount. Apparently, they had worked it out. She asked him what his name was and was told "Storm". Greylin wondered what his full name might be. She didn't want to push, though, but he must have guessed her desire and said, "He was named Cobalt's Darkling Firestorm."

"That's beautiful. Is Cobalt a stable or a lineage?"

"Both. Sort of. There are three bloodlines recorded in *Bloodlines of the Friesian Horse* that was written by King Abelon Hilde, one of your ancestors I would assume. One is Cobalt, the others are Starfire and Darklight. For some reason, I always get Cobalt's descendants, though there's some Darklight mixed in with Storm. Cobalt foals tend to bc fcisty, Darklight's are more mellow."

She grew quiet then. She was stirring up memories she didn't want him tortured with.

Storm did prove to be more mellow. He walked along with half-closed eyes and always stood quietly when they stopped. She wondered what he'd be like in battle. She couldn't picture him moving fast never mind killing anyone, certainly not with the ferocity she had seen in Bane, but she got a glimpse of his power as they rode along.

A bee started buzzing around them. They ignored it, but it wouldn't leave. One second it was buzzing around Storm's head and then—*flick! Snap!*—and it was gone. Storm continued on with half-closed eyes. D'Arcannon chuckled.

"Did you see that?" Greylin exclaimed.

"Yes. He's fast, I'll give him that," D'Arcannon replied with the half-smile coming back to his face.

"So fast I hardly saw it! He struck faster than a snake!" she replied.

They reached Tower Grace later that day. The Camp had been ready for the onslaught thanks to Finn warning them ahead of time, and they had done well. There were fewer attacking them than what they had dealt with at Adelia, and the reinforcements helped mainly with cleanup. In fact, it was hard to tell a battle had even taken place!

Greylin asked for Finn and was told that he left the same day after delivering his message. No one had seen him on the road, and he never returned to Fort Adelia.

What happened to him? After double-checking with everyone who might have encountered him and finding out little more, they decided to ride back towards Tower Adelia and look for clues. Greylin was becoming more and more worried. Late in the day, they stopped by one of Castabal's many ponds to water the horses and have something to eat.

While they were resting, a girl watched them hesitantly from the opposite shore. They smiled and nodded. She lingered and seemed to want to talk, but was too shy and afraid, probably of the men. They were very intimidating to a country girl, Greylin could swear to that. *Perhaps,* Greylin thought, *she will be less afraid of me,* so she wandered down the bank. Sure enough.

"Miss," the girl called.

"Yes?"

"Did you, or did someone, lose a horse? Do you know?"

"Perhaps," Greylin answered, her heart pounding.

"What kind of horse?"

"It was walking up the road with a saddle on, the reins were dragging. I wanted to keep him, but father said it was a fine horse and must belong to someone. A lot of people rode by a couple days ago but didn't stop. You were the first I could ask."

And the first you weren't afraid of, Greylin thought.

"Can you bring him to us?"

"Yes. I will. Wait here," she said and ran off. Greylin went back to the others.

"She said she found a horse—with no rider. You don't think it could be Finn's, do you?"

"We'll be able to tell once we see it." D'Arcannon said.

A few minutes later, the girl returned. She had even managed to saddle the horse. Their faces fell as soon as they looked at it. Not only was it the same horse, but the sword and scabbard of the short sword D'Arcannon had given Greylin and Finn had borrowed was looped over the saddle horn. They rewarded the girl with five gold coins for her honesty. The horse, tack, or sword would have brought her and her family a small fortune had she sold them.

Greylin began to fear the worst. "Where is he? What could have happened?"

Finn was the one person she hadn't worried about— the one she thought was safe! *Why did I send him here? This is all my fault. I've made a terrible mistake. Why didn't I use the crown before volunteering him? Where could he be?*

Something must have happened to him on his way back, but they didn't know exactly where. The girl, Jonea her name was, told them there were no known robbers or highwaymen in the area, and that the roads were safe to travel. There were no regular patrols, however, and that may have changed.

Greylin knew Hollinghast had the ability to scry, and she asked him if he could scry for Finn. The tall mage stood with his staff before him. At its top was a perfectly round crystal. Sometimes it was clear, sometimes murky, and sometimes it seemed to be full of a milky, swirling fog. He sang low, then high, an eerie, wistful song that called to her, tugging at her heart. The small globe cleared then there was what looked to her like a tiny arrowswift gliding ahead. *It's like a compass,* she thought, *it points to whoever you're looking for!*

Hollinghast carefully mounted Merelda, still holding the staff before him, and trotted off across a field. He was led to the west. D'Arcannon and Greylin followed his lead but by nightfall they had found nothing.

The mage tried again the next day by himself, stating that he could move faster on his own. He returned dejected. "I can't locate him," he said, rubbing his tired eyes, "and I don't understand what I'm following. We go round and round, back and forth, and where it seems to fixate, there is nothing. Just grass and trees. It could be a false indication, I have no explanation for that, but I don't think I am going to find him this way."

"I don't understand," Greylin said.

"I don't either, truly. I'll keep trying though."

Greylin remembered animals that would go missing on the farm she shared with Daara. Sometimes, no matter how hard they searched, they could never find any trace of them. It was always frustrating, sad, and there would never be any resolution. They would never know what happened to them. Some part of Greylin was always looking for them as she went about her chores, especially if it was one she cared deeply about. It was maddening. She wanted to run and find Finn, but she had no idea where to go.

She tried on the Crown that night to try to find him. She took first watch because she told them she couldn't sleep anyway. All she could see was darkness. She heard something, but it could have been anything, from her own blood rushing through her veins to the stream behind her. *Does the darkness mean he is dead?* She pulled the Crown off and held her head in her hands in frustration.

Chapter 30

A CHANGE OF TACTICS

*"The greatest evil is one that is
perpetrated by the flatterer."*

-*THE BETRAYER,* A PLAY BY THE
BARD OF CHILLISTON ABBEY

Archcanon Jaarven Hilde sat still as stone in the quiet of his study. None of his plans had met with success. *Why, oh why, wouldn't that girl just die?* he wondered. It was always the case: The one person whose death would solve all the conflicts, all the problems, just lived on and on to a ripe old age while hundreds, sometimes thousands fell to their deaths. History was full of examples: Tyrants, weak kings, invaders, and now this little devil spawn of a girl. He had waited too long to act. *How long has it been? Ten years? More?* he wondered, since he began to take over every aspect of the king's duties and privileges. *I waited too long. I became complacent.*

He sighed. The sound was so loud in the quiet it nearly echoed.

It had been weeks since he was visited by the whispers. *Weeks!* He grew more morose with each passing day. Even as he indulged in his misery, he thought he heard a soft sigh. He listened intently—there it was again, that soft sighing sound as though a paper had fallen off his desk. He sat back, eyes closed and waited.

Soon a feathery touch caressed his cheek.

"Hiiilllde," it whispered.

"I am here," he replied. He always did even though it must be obvious that he was.

"Do not despaaiirr," it whispered.

"I don't know what else to do," he said. "Everything I have attempted has failed."

"Befriend," it whispered.

"Beguile," it continued.

"Betray," it breathed.

Quiet descended on the room. Had he heard right? He must have, it was so simple. So easy. *Befriend, beguile, betray.*

The silence was broken by laughter.

Chapter 31

RETURNS

*"Our magic is made of song and our songs make
magic, so much so we sometimes forget that there are
other forms of magic, many of which are made with
the hands and which are no less powerful".*

-THE WHITE MAGE OF TAIVASTA

Greylin's small party arrived in Rimmon two days
later. Greeted as heroes, which they surely were, a great
banquet was prepared in celebration. Tents were erected
and long tables laid out. Cooks toiled from morning to
night preparing the best of their cuisine to feed the soldiers.
Beer, ale, mead, and wine flowed freely. Song and dance
were the order of the day and the plainbards were treated
to much food and drink as well. At last, toward evening as
a few exhausted revelers were seen sleeping in surprising
places, the music mellowed and slowed.

Greylin made her final visit with the Golden Brigade,
grateful for their help and sad to say goodbye as they
cheered her. A few minutes later, Captain Redmond found
her sitting by a fountain, staring pensively at the black,
orange, and white fish within. She noticed his approach
and turned to him.

Captain Redmond saluted her and with a deferential
nod of his head said, "M'lady, we depart in the morning
with your leave."

"Of course," she replied.

He looked ruefully around at the carousing men and
continued, "but perhaps not too early."

The laughed together. Greylin said, "I will miss you. I
am indebted to you for your service to me and to this land.

It was nothing I was entitled to, yet for all of Allanda, we prevailed."

"We did indeed."

"I have released you and your men from their vows and bid you good speed on your journey home. I have no means of my own to reward you, but I hear that my uncle has done so generously."

"He has at that. I will tell you, however, that even though you have released us, we will return if you need us. The men..." he paused, searching for words, "see you as a friend to Sessirra. I fear—if I may speak freely?"

"Please do, Captain!"

"You may have need of us again. There are rumors and suspicions. All does not seem well in Taivasta. The king falters while another grows stronger, and pretends there is no army, yet garrisons are erected and manned along the border between Taivasta and Sessirra. As you know, Sessirra is a rich city though we are small by comparison. Our riches may tempt a greedy man."

Greylin's eyes widened. She knew who he meant, it could only be Jaarven, but Redmond was too discreet to mention his name aloud.

"I see," she said finally. "I hope it will not come to... conflict." She didn't want to say "war", shrinking from the thought

"If it does," Redmond said in a quiet voice, "we will align with you. Call for us and we will come."

He handed her an eversilver token stamped with the insignia of two overlapping circles pierced with an upright sword. "Just send this."

She took the token in astonishment, "When did you—and how?"

He laughed. "We are not soldiers by trade, remember, there are metalsmiths among us."

She clutched the token in her hand as a wave of premonition shuddered through her.

"Thank you, Captain Redmond. I am honored beyond words. May I always be worthy of your good opinion. You and your men."

He bowed again. "So be it. Until we meet again."
She watched him until he disappeared from view.

***

Greylin's uncle treated her and her friends once again to his generous hospitality. He asked if there was anything he could do for her, and she asked for two things. First, if she could keep the armor. He laughed delightedly and said it was already hers and pressed her to ask for more. Then she asked if they could have Rilann accompany them north. He happily granted this request as well, telling her he was in their service for as long as they both chose.

D'Arcannon and Hollinghast looked at Greylin as though she must have lost her mind. *Why Rilann?* they wondered. But she had a good reason: she missed Rilah's companionship terribly while they were gone. Greylin had grown used to her help and advice. It was worse now that Finn was not to be found. Greylin missed his friendship, and it hurt keenly. She also didn't want to separate brother and sister now that they had finally found each other, so if Rilann came along, Rilah would be happier. And if he didn't have a girlfriend, well, being along wouldn't hurt.

Rilah, anticipating Greylin's needs and practical as always, had secretly asked the queen for clothes for Greylin, knowing she had hardly any. Packed into a wagon of supplies were hand-me-down gowns and riding attire the women of the castle had outgrown. The queen apologized profusely because they did not have time to make new ones for her, but Rilah was adamant that they had done her a great service.

One day, the king requested their presence in his private chamber. He had just received an arrowswift with a formal invitation for Greylin to return to New Saar. It was signed and sealed with the Archcanon's personal stamp which Hollinghast and D'Arcannon confirmed as legitimate having seen it far too many times.

"To the Princess Cianalas Hiraeth di Castillo Hilde," the king read aloud. He arched an eyebrow, "Seems you have won favor in high places."

"Or low places," D'Arcannon quipped.

They laughed.

"And also," the king continued, "To her esteemed companions Heron Hannes Hollinghast, Master Mage of the Lumerian Order, Bard of Eminent Merit, bearer of the Star of Valor and Tree of Valkoinen, and Reist Denali D'Arcannon, Paladin of the Mazarine Order, Champion of the Palonen, and Knight of the Order of the Lion.

"Proves my point," D'Arcannon laughed.

"He's laying it on a bit thick," Hollinghast said.

"I didn't know you had middle names," Greylin said. "What am I saying? I didn't even know *I* had a middle name!"

They laughed.

Hollinghast looked sheepish and bowed, "I apologize. I forgot what it was."

This brought more laughter.

The king continued, "The royal family of Hilde extends a most welcome invitation to the court of King Sterren Einaren Hilde at your earliest convenience to honor the return and accomplishments of the Princess and reunite her with her family… and it goes on and on with nonsense. So, what do you think of that?"

Greylin's eyes widened, Hollinghast stroked his chin, D'Arcannon grimaced and finally said, "It could be a trap."

Hollinghast said, "But we're bound to go anyway."

"I can see this has caused great rejoicing among you," the king said, dryly. "Please feel free to stay here as long as you like."

*　*　*

The next evening before dinner as they gathered in the family room Greylin approached the king. He welcomed her to sit near him and after settling in she said, "I never knew my mother, nor have I met anyone who knew her well."

"And you would like to know more about her," he finished.

"Yes. I don't know what to think. I don't understand how what happened... happened," she said.

"I can tell you that she was beautiful, but that you probably know. As to how such a thing could happen, there are two things that brought it about. The first is her ability in magic. She was superb. When we were learning spells, she always beat us and then laughed while we fumbled through. It came so easily to her."

"Why then, would she go to a place that is so against a woman using magic"?" Greylin asked.

"I'm sure she thought it wouldn't matter. It was none of "their" business. That's where the other factor came in. She was—how can I put this—" he sighed. "Snobbish? I guess you would call it that. She felt superior. She despised those she called "peasants" and would have nothing to do with the members of the lesser houses. It was a bit of a relief when she left to tell you the truth. Who would marry her? It would have to be a king, nothing else would do. So there was Sterren in Taivasta, and she would consider no one else. None of our great families would do. She had managed to insult them all over the years. So she brought that attitude north along with a careless attitude to creating spells, and is it a surprise that she wasn't liked? Hardly. This does not excuse what happened to her. That was brutal and barbaric."

Greylin dropped her eyes. She felt somehow responsible and embarrassed by the behavior of the country that would be her birthright.

"I cannot fathom how she did what she did. Something must have changed. She must have been very lonely, more than anyone realized. Who was Daavin D'Arcannon to her?" He darted a look at Reist D'Arcannon sitting across the room entertaining the children with silly antics. He hoped he hadn't heard.

Greylin followed his look with her eyes. *I think I could hazard a guess,* she thought.

***

Greylin was in no hurry to leave, and every time the subject of departing came up, she stalled for another day. She was fascinated with the castle and would wander its halls peeking into rooms from open doorways, astonished at how different each one was and how beautiful.

One day as she was wandering in the afternoon, she turned down a hallway she hadn't noticed before. Light was shining from a lowering sun through a window beside a winding stone staircase. She climbed it to look out of the window. The view was one of hundreds of miles of low green hills separated by lakes, ponds, streams, and canals that were crossed with bridges wide and narrow.

Another window higher up glowed with light and she walked up to look out of that one for a slightly higher view. The staircase was within a turret that jutted out from the castle wall. Beyond that, the stair turned, and she could see a doorway that also glowed with light. She was drawn by the brightness and entered a room with rows of windows high and low that flooded the room with golden light. At the far end, an old woman sat. Greylin would not have noticed her if it were not for the movement of the woman's hands as she worked on a piece of embroidery.

"Hello," the woman said, smiling at her. "I've been waiting for you."

She's been waiting for me? "Hello," Greylin replied and walked over to her.

The woman was much smaller than Greylin, and her hands were fine-boned, though wrinkled and a bit knobby. She was dressed in an elaborately embroidered gown that blended in with the chair she was sitting in as well as the pillows all around her, all of which were covered in silken threads depicting flowers, vines, animals, and geometric trellises.

"Sit," the woman said and motioned to a padded stool.
"You are Cianalas," she said.

Greylin started, "Yes," she replied. She was rarely called by her given name and it surprised her.

"Do you know what that means?" the woman smiled brightly over her handwork.

"I...no I guess I don't." *I didn't know it meant anything*, Greylin thought to herself.

"It's a good word, a good name, though a sad one. It describes a deep homesickness. A yearning for home in the deepest sense of the word. Our real home, where we belong, perhaps even beyond this one, one we almost remember that is full of peace, warmth, love, and contentment. The opposite of this world of strife."

Her words stirred something deep in Greylin, and she found it hard to speak. Finally, she managed to ask, "Who are you? I haven't seen you at dinner."

"Oh, that's too much excitement for me. I keep to myself in peace where I can do my work. I'm your great-grandmother, Linnea Linna, on your grandmother's side."

"Oh! No one told me. I am glad to meet you!"

"And I, you," she said as she pulled out a pair of tiny scissors and cut a thread. "Here, I made this for you. You must always wear it. It will protect you," she said and lifted up a sash of violet and silver that was covered with delicate silken thread in patterns that seemed to slide away from Greylin's eyes.

Greylin accepted it graciously, stood and placed it around her hips. It fit perfectly and she admired the panel in front.

"Don't worry," her great-grandmother said, patting the sash with one birdlike hand. Her eyes twinkling brightly. "There is more going on than meets the eye! People always underestimate ELIEL, and even St. Rauna for that matter, as though they didn't have any part to play, yet the threads of life are everywhere."

She laughed a musical laugh like a young girl then and put away her sewing.

"You should show this to Oro," she continued, "Now go on or you'll be late for dinner."

"Thank you, Grandmother. It is beautiful!" Greylin stood and impulsively hugged the tiny woman before taking her leave.

Later after they had eaten another sumptuous feast, the king was enjoying a thin-stemmed white pipe near a fireplace by himself. Greylin approached and showed him the sash. She had concealed it beneath a shawl the queen had given her, not quite knowing why she hid it, perhaps to keep the memory of her meeting with her great-grandmother to herself like a treasured gem.

When he saw it, he paled.

"Where did you get that?" he asked, visibly shaken.

"From Great Grandmother Linnea, she said I should show you."

He looked up at her, wide-eyed, and said, "Come with me."

He led her through a private study to a locked cabinet and pulled a key from his belt. He unlocked it, took a small box from a shelf and opened it with yet another key. Inside was an identical sash.

"Oh!" Greylin said, "it's just like mine. Did she make that for you?"

"Many years ago. I was only eight years old, and I climbed a forgotten stair that glowed in the setting sun and found her working in an upstairs room. She gave this to me, and I brought it back proudly to my parents. They asked me where I found it, and I told them. They didn't believe me, and punished me, making me stay in my room for a week, but they let me keep it."

"Why didn't they believe you? They could have just asked her!" Greylin said.

"Linnea Linna," he nodded his head toward a painting of a lovely young woman, "died over 100 years ago. She's your great, great, great, great grandmother."

Greylin looked at him in shock.

"I started to believe I had dreamt it. You restored my belief that it truly happened. Thank you. I will wear it always now, as she asked. If I had any doubts that you were my niece, I no longer have them."

The next day and the day after that Greylin tried to find the staircase again and couldn't.

Chapter 32

NEW SAAR

*"It is a daring thing to leave one's home for an
extended journey, for if you return, it never
looks quite the same."*

- PRINCESS CIANALAS OF NEW SAAR,
LETTERS

If her friends hadn't pushed her, Greylin might have
turned her back on New Saar and stayed in Rimmon. She
was happy there. This time there was no rush to travel from
one place to another at a frantic pace. There was time to
say goodbye, time to plan, prepare, and perhaps too much
time to worry. Greylin was beginning to question things
again. The crown showed her a safe welcome in New Saar
but not much beyond that. While that might have seemed
reassuring on one hand, it also meant that anything she said
or did might change things in any unexpected direction.

Money was no object; King Castillo rewarded them
generously for their help against the Jonjishalan. He had
tried to talk Greylin into staying and she almost conceded.
Instead she promised to return if things did not go well.

Once again, they formed a small party: Hollinghast,
D'Arcannon, Greylin, Rilann and Rilah. The absence of
Finn was keenly felt. They left Castabal and crossed into
Taivasta, stopping at Trolldale, the first town across the
border. The lumpy hills were known for harboring trolls,
thus the town's name and the name of the Trollhammer
Inn.

Settling into the pub area was a squeeze. A popular
plainbard—non-magical singer—had been drawing a
crowd. He was taking a break and being treated to drinks

from some of the patrons. Some of the early comers left and they were able to find an empty table. The Trollhammer was bustling with news about the Jonji attack. The conversations around them were mixed, and they sat quietly and listened to the talk.

"They say that Castabal asked for help and the king turned them down," a scrawny young man said.

"They should have asked the Archcanon. He's the only one who does anything. The king is a do-nothing," his burly companion replied.

"That's not what I heard. I heard it was the Archcanon who advised the king to say no," piped up a woman with them.

"You don't know that," the burly man said and continued, "It's the Archcanon who does everything. He makes sure the roads are repaired, the drains are being fixed. It's his people who collect the taxes and make it happen."

Hollinghast and D'Arcannon exchanged glances. *Since when did he take over tax collection?* their expressions said.

"I heard some girl claimed she was the princess an' it's her to thank for stopping those monsters at the strait," the woman said.

"She'll have a fight on her hands then," the bigger man said.

"Why?" asked the scrawny one.

The big man laughed, "He's not going to let some interlopin' skirt come in and make waves. He already took care o' that. Passed a law, he did," the big man nodded in satisfaction as though he'd won an argument hands down.

Greylin slid a little lower in her seat. She glanced at Rilah who looked at her with sympathy and touched her hand. A few days ago, soldiers were kissing her hand and pledging loyalty. Now she was being maligned as an interloper in Taivasta before even arriving there. The innkeeper—who looked a little troll-like himself with a bulbous nose and squinty eyes—brought over their meal of rabbit stew and fresh bread.

"Sorry there was no roast beef left. We've been so busy since the wars on the coast," he said.

They're calling them wars now? she thought.

"I'm sure the food is excellent. You have a nice place here. What do you hear of the wars then?" D'Arcannon asked, turning on the dazzling smile.

The Innkeeper beamed and told them a garbled version of what had happened: The Jonji attacked and got all the way to Rimmon. An army of volunteers banded together to fight them and managed to keep them down south. King Castillo is trying to pass off one of his nieces as the daughter of King Sterren. He had her lead the army because he's a coward and wanted to make her look legitimate.

D'Arcannon complimented the food and dragged every last bit of gossip from the man.

Greylin looked like she was going to be ill.

"It's best to know what we're up against," D'Arcannon whispered.

"Don't worry. They talk a lot but they change opinions like the wind changes direction," Hollinghast chimed in.

Greylin didn't know what awaited her in New Saar, but instinctively she knew her life would change as completely as it had the day she left Maddy Sedge. In fact, the only enticement that worked on her was that they said they would travel by way of Maddy Sedge and she could see Daara.

It took a week of travel to get there. When they approached Maddy Sedge, they reached the village first. *Was it always so shabby?* she wondered. The cluster of buildings that was once the center of her life seemed small and unattractive now. She had been to two beautiful cities, cities that took her breath away with their grandeur and beauty: Sessirra and Rimmon. In comparison, Maddy Sedge lost all its appeal. She didn't want to seem snobbish, but nevertheless she felt strangely embarrassed by it—or more likely embarrassed by her former opinion of it. So much had happened! It was only a few months, yet she had grown by leaps and bounds, so much so it was like years—like a lifetime.

They rode through the village and a few boys gathered around and watched, dumbstruck, as they passed, and then ran after them for a while. Greylin remembered their names. She didn't want them to realize who she was, and thought, correctly, that with the original obscuration spell removed, they wouldn't even recognize her. In truth, she wasn't that person anymore. She had grown at least a two-and-a-half hands once the restricting spell was removed, her hair had grown below her shoulders, and almost daily sword practice had built muscles of twice the size of what she had only months before.

As they approached the farm, her feelings eased. Here were the trees, fields, and ponds that she remembered so fondly. They approached the yard and she could see the edge of the barn roof now and the chimney on the house. She urged Roki into a trot and entered the yard.

No one was there, no animals wandered through the yard, no chickens were pecking at the ground or chasing flies. The fields were neglected, the garden was overgrown, and part of the roof had fallen in. *Where was Daara?* The one good sign was that the water bucket was upside down on the top of the hand-pumped well—that was the signal to the neighbors that she wasn't home—intentionally. Greylin hoped she was still at Lindström's Farm with Bild and Miza.

"I have to find Daara. If she's where she was heading when we left, it's quicker to cut across fields. That way." She pointed east.

"Lead the way," Hollinghast replied, and they urged their horses into a mile-eating lope.

In short order, they thundered into the Lindström's farmyard and to her relief, Daara was hanging clothes out on a line. Greylin jumped off Roki and ran up to her and threw her arms around her.

Daara looked at her strangely and backed up a bit.

"Who are you?" she asked.

"It's me. Grae. Do I look that different?"

Daara nodded hesitantly. "You can't be. Grae can't talk."

"That spell was taken off. It cured me but I had to learn how."

Daara squinted at her. "You look so different I didn't recognize you. I can't get used to it." She looked down at her laundry. "It is me. Where's Bild and Miza?"

"They went to Madhia to sell some produce and wool." What happened to the farm?"

Daara shrugged her shoulders. "There didn't seem any point to keeping the farm going without Grae—you—there. The Lindströms invited me to stay. We built a cottage addition on the side here, so I have my own space. We help each other. The animals mix. We still use the fields at the old place sometimes, but I don't live there. In fact, we're looking for a tenant."

Daara was shy and distant. Greylin wanted things to be the same. She wanted to slip into her old life for a moment, shed all the worries and anxieties, and just be "Grae the farm boy" for a while, but it was like trying to fit into a too-small shoe. Had she really fought with this woman because she wanted to go off into the wide world and fight battles? Daara looked so small and frail to her now. She hugged her.

"I'm glad you are alright. I was worried—I didn't know if trouble would find you after we left."

"Oh, I'm fine. Happy really. I have the Lindströms for help and the work goes so much smoother. It was hard for just the two of us. I see that now. Look here, I'm not being a good host. Come in. Have something to eat."

She was still talking to Greylin like she was a stranger. *Maybe I am,* Greylin thought. She almost suggested that they move on, but she knew that once Daara became more comfortable, she would want to know all that happened. She also knew that she got on well with Hollinghast, so she would let him do most of the talking.

As usual, Daara managed to come up with enough food and drink for everyone. Greylin had forgotten how good her cooking was. When Daara wasn't looking Greylin tucked a few gold coins around the house. They ate a lot, and Greylin wanted her to be able to replace it. She knew she wouldn't take the money if offered.

"Daara, I have a question for you," Greylin asked as they finished their repast. "The mark of the House of Hilde. The cup-shaped birthmark. I don't think I have it. Do I?"

Daara's face changed. Greylin knew that expression all too well, it had appeared every time she tried to ask a question that Daara didn't want to answer. Greylin's ability to talk had been taken from her at an early age by Daara's husband, and Daara would often pretend she didn't know what Greylin was asking. Greylin would bruise her hands, slamming them on the table in frustration. Daara's expression showed a combination of anger and fear, and something else, a blankness Greylin couldn't put a name to.

"I don't remember," Daara snapped.

Hollinghast stepped in gently, "I think you might. Try."

Daara's eyes seemed to go in separate directions, her mouth moving in a twitch. Greylin had only seen that happen occasionally when she pushed too hard for answers. It was unnerving and had usually put an end to the discussion, as it did now. If Daara knew, they would not be able to get it out of her. She was likely to die of a fit before then.

"Nevermind, Daara. It's okay," Greylin said, soothingly.

Later on, Greylin asked Hollinghast if Daara's strange behavior was because of a spell. He shook his head in the negative and said it was something that Daara had created herself and that only she could choose to change it.

It wasn't until they rode away that Greylin realized she might have compromised Daara's safety. Hollinghast told her when they left the first time that it was better that he not know where Daara was in case the king asked. Greylin voiced those concerns to him.

He said, "There's more than one way to answer a question." When she pressed, he said, "The woman Sarra Duplessy had the girl on a farm. She isn't living there anymore. She's gone away." Greylin could see that if she asked him a question in the future, she'd have to be very thorough if she wanted all the answers!

"I keep thinking about Finn," Greylin said as they walked along. "I suppose we should tell his mother."

Hollinghast peered down at her. "I sent an arrowswift to the Valkoinen Hall in Sessirra. They will let her know."

"I don't even know her name!" Greylin wailed. "How inconsiderate is that? I never asked. She was just there. And now…"

"Her name is Oshaya Reed. Selkan women don't take their husband's names. I told her Finn was missing but not in battle."

Greylin's face fell and she bit her bottom lip.

***

All too soon they traversed the Dolar Plains. They were flat and seemed endless, but so fertile. It was summer's end and every tree and plant was bowed down with vegetables, fruit, nuts or berries. For once they did not hurry. They would make camp by the road, or at a shelter, and even had time to take leisurely walks and spend some time talking. The only shadow on their minds was the fact that they still worried about Finn.

Then one day, the whole of New Saar was before them: sitting squat and thick behind a protective wall that was fringed with crenellations along the top like lace trim on a pie pan. D'Arcannon pointed out Kyynel Island on the Halla River, Castle Hilde on the right of it just peeking above the edge, and Kurok Tower at the center of the Red Gaol—the infamous Kurok Tower of Traitor's Gate— which was, ironically, it's most attractive feature. The other Great Halls peeked over the wall, the Palatine, the Lumerian Hall, the Rose Cathedral, and the Healer's Temple.

Greylin had one flash of memory, and it was of a city that was more of a town made of hurried buildings and muddy streets. It had grown, but she had not seen its growth, so she had no memory of it.

They stopped for the night at the King's Crossing Inn so they could wash and dress appropriately for the next day. Greylin thanked ELIEL again, and not for the last time, for the presence of Rilah to help her. She was so nervous she didn't know what she would have done without her. Rilann announced that he was leaving to go back to Rimmon but would be back "to spy on them" soon.

There were three bridges, the King's Bridge which they would cross; the other two were the Merchant's Bridge and the Warrior's Way. The guards did not challenge them, the gates were open, and they entered uneventfully and made their way to the castle.

This can't be happening, Greylin thought. *After all this time, it doesn't seem real. I feel as though I am in a dream stranger than the visions I have.*

They approached the King's Bridge and a rat came running out from their left and raced across the road chased by a large black cat. The rat hesitated which spelled its doom as the cat pounced and bit it and carried it away, its limp legs hanging and twitching. Not a good omen, Greylin thought. She saw another cat sitting on the wall of the bridge and as they entered New Saar she saw two or three more. *The rat wasn't, but maybe all these cats are.*

"Why are there so many cats?" she asked.

D'Arcannon answered, "New Saar had a rat problem. Or has a rat problem, as you saw. They encourage the cats."

They do indeed, she thought. They were walking along a gray cobblestone street and to one side she saw a pile of sand set off by a square of wooden boards. One cat was just exiting and took off running down the street. There were cats everywhere she looked. Not more than people but enough to make her think of it as the City of Cats.

"The only place they don't go is the Rose Cathedral. That tells you a lot," he continued.

"That's only because they chase them away," Hollinghast added.

When they got to the Castle Gate, they were challenged by the Castle Guard dressed in crisp black and gold livery. Hollinghast identified himself and waved the invitation that had been sent by the Archcanon. Apparently, their arrival was anticipated because they were rapidly ushered into the King's throne room and Greylin braced herself to meet her father.

End of Book II

Greylin's saga continues in

BOOK III: THE CHALICE ROSE

APPENDICES

Appendix I
List of new characters in order of appearance. Main characters from Book I are in Appendix III.

Capt. Skerry Skellig - Cousin to Finn Skellig and captain of the *Windracer* out of Sessirra. He is given to dramatic storytelling and tall tales.

Sir Mikhael Harras - Warrior Knight of the Mazarine Order. A trusted and capable warrior often chosen for missions vital to the Mazarines.

Lord Tarkea Blackthorne, P.E. (for Paladin Emeritus) - the second son of the House of Blackthorne, one of the great houses. He married Amita Pali and lost his paladin powers. He has been the head of the Mazarine Order in New Saar for seven years. He is a large, black-haired, copper-skinned man, brother to Kota Blackthorne, who is a Canon of the Vermilion Order, and whose booming voice he shares as a family trait.

Duren Karhu - a Lumerian page working in the arrowswift aviary in New Saar

Iva Fontannen - Lumerian acolyte assistant in aviary and grounds in New Saar.

Kofee Saley and Ito Ishiki - Lumerian masters in New Saar.

King Sterren Einaren Hilde - king of Taivasta and father to the Princess Cianalas Hiraeth Hilde daughter of the executed Queen Isabela di Castillo Hilde. His current queen, Lyda, has born no children.

Koren and Sato - two of the people living on the island of Edda. They are the mother and father of Rilann Blake and his twin sister Rilah who chooses to leave the island and go with Greylin to the mainland.

Captain Everlan Redmond - leader of the Golden Brigade out of Sessirra

Oro Develen di Xanchez Castillo - King of Castabal and sister to Isabela di Castillo, Greylin's mother, which makes him Greylin's uncle. He is a charming, generous, and fair king. So beloved of his people, that they nicknamed him the Day Star.

Sergei Illyich - King Castillo's Captain of the Horseguard

Tauro Sandovar - King Castillo's General of the Army

Garron - King Castillo's Lord High Steward, a tall, elegant man entrusted with running the castle

Queen Vittoria - King Oro Castillo's queen

Lady Serenia - Sister to Queen Vittoria

King Castillo's children:
Valentin - a baby, a few months old
Virdiana - three
Darien - five
Lumin - seven
Serafina - ten
Romana twelve, the oldest and likely heiress to the throne

Commander Rayne Salazar - In charge of Tower Adelia in Castabal

Linnea Linna – One of the greatest queens of Castabal who helped design Torilinna castle.

Queen Lyda Hilde - the gracious queen of Taivasta, married to King Sterren Hilde. She has no children.

Storm – a large, sleek, black Friesian with a quiet disposition when not fighting but a swift and fierce opponent when he is.

Appendix II

Some notes on pronunciation Gentle Reader, you can pronounce these names however you like. If you would like to know how I "hear" them, though, I have listed some of the trickier ones here. Know that many names and words are in Finnish so the accent will always be on the first syllable and not the second.

Place Names:
Taivasta (TIE-vast-ah) – The middle kingdom whose capital is New Saar

Castabal (CAST-ah-bell) – The southernmost kingdom whose capital is Rimmon

Lumenvalo (LU-men-VAL-oh) – The northernmost kingdom whose capital is Ryysylainen

Sessirra (SESSir-ah) – The westernmost city closely aligned with Taivasta but not ruled by them or by a king. It is the largest seaport in Allanda and is controlled by merchants

Allanda (al-AND-ah) – Encompasses the known world (It doesn't follow that general rule of accent placement like the others because it is not a Finnish word.)

Moons:
Enshallah – en-SHALL-ah the middle moon
Dedira – da-DEER-ah the largest moon **Aníramie** – ah-NIR-ah-me the smallest moon
Luma – LU-mah the sun

Character Names: Double "aa" sounds like the "a" in "father" for Daara, Saar, Daavin, Jaarven, haapa
The "au" sounds like the "ow" in cow
for Rauna – ROW-nah, and Aulis – OWL-is

Cianalas (chee-AN-ah-LASS) – A Gaelic word meaning homesickness, a longing for the place of one's roots, attributed to the Outer Hebrides Hiraeth (hee-RIETH) – A Welsh word meaning a homesick longing for a place that might never have been, such as the Shire in The Lord of the Rings

Reist – Rhymes with feist, heist and Christ

Unusual items and words
Chantsinging – A combination of song and chanting akin to Gregorian chants used in spellcasting
Fisal (FIE-sel) – a small tasty fish similar to haddock and cod
Groundmite – A predatory lizard similar to a komodo dragon
Haapa tree – An aspen type of tree with a soft wood used for many things including making paper, its leaves are on flat stems and rustle with the slightest breeze
Kaani (KON-ee) – A rabbit-sized, game animal
Kantele (KON-tell-ay) – a Finnish instrument similar to a zither
Kantelyre (KON-tell-ire) – a smaller version of a kantele easily slung over the shoulder and across the chest on a strap **Loitsusäilö** (LOIT-su-SIE-lo) – translates as "spell storage"
Malja Ruusu (MAL-ya RUE-sue) – translates roughly as "chalice rose" **Nähdä Pahaa** (NAH-da PAH-ha) – translates "to see evil"
Slinkhound – a type of canine similar to a hyena in appearance

Appendix III

<u>List of Main Characters</u>
In order of their appearance in Book One *The Sword Argente*

Isabela Castillo – known as the Witch Queen of Taivasta, she came from the southern country of Castabal to marry King Sterren Hilde. She had one daughter, Cianalas Hiraeth Hilde, before being executed for the crime of high treason by reason of her love affair with Daavin D'Arcannon. She is sister to the King of Castabal and was one of the most beautiful women in all of Allanda. She had dark hair, dark eyes, and graceful movements. She was adept at magic and headstrong, which ultimately led to her downfall.

Daara Dupin / Sarra Duplessy – One-time nurse companion to Queen Isabela. Sarra went to Taivasta with the future queen when she married King Sterren Hilde. She disappeared on the day of Isabela's execution and was thought to have kidnapped the baby princess. She changed her name to Daara and married a man with the last name of Dupin. Saara's greatest attribute is loyalty. She loved Isabela and continued to bestow that love on Greylin. She is a plump, mousey, unimaginative woman, but generally fearful and distrustful of others which was confirmed for her with Isabela's death.

Greylin – a girl of the village of Maddy Sedge who is cared for by her "aunt" Daara. She is disguised as a boy and is known as Grae. She looks, moves, and dresses like a boy and has dun-colored hair and eyes and skin. She is initially unable to speak but is expressive with gestures. She does not know who her parents are and Daara has never explained. Her last name might be Dupin, or perhaps it is Hilde if she is the lost princess of Taivasta. If so, her full name would be Cianalas Hiraeth Hilde. If not, she could just be an orphan farm girl disguised as a boy by the muddled servant of a doomed queen. Either way, someone is trying to kill her. Greylin is the name she goes by, and she isn't in search of an identity; she's in search of a sword that appears to her in dreams and visions.

Heron Hannes Hollinghast – Master Mage of the Lumerian Order, Bard of Eminent Merit, Bearer of the Star of Valor and Tree of Valkoinen. He is the son of Henri Hollinghast and Anna Blackthorne Hollinghast of Langwer, owners of the Holling Eversilver mines. He is extremely adept at chantsinging spells due to his exceptionally melodious voice, and while he can play various instruments, he prefers a magical kantelyre made from the jawbone of a sea pike. He and Reist D'Arcannon have been close friends since childhood. He is exceptionally tall and thin with a long straight nose, high cheekbones and deep-set eyes. He has white hair to his shoulders and a white trimmed beard. These have faded due to the use of magic. His eyes have also faded to a light blue. He also carries a white ashwood staff.

Reist Denali D'Arcannon – Paladin of the Mazarine Order, Champion of the Palonen, and Knight of the Order of the Lion. He is the son of Renaud D'Arcannon and Tarora Haka D'Arcannon of Langwer, owners of the Darcon Iron Mines. He is also younger brother to the disgraced and executed Daavin D'Arcannon. He is heavily muscled and dark-skinned, favoring the Haka clan. He has dark brown eyes and black hair cropped short, and his beard close-shaved both of which is a characteristic of paladin status and require no tending. He carries a long sword, crossbow, and dagger.

Archcanon Jaarven Vissarian Bortig Hilde – Halfbrother to the older King Sterren Hilde, ruler of Taivasta, Jaarven worked his way up through the ranks of priests to become the head of the Church of the Covenant in Taivasta. His driving force is ambition, however, rather than devotion. He is an outstanding administrator and resents the fate that placed him below what he sees as his incompetent brother. His resentment and envy have opened him to evil influences. He is portly with brown eyes and hair, his bangs cut to his eyebrows and the length trimmed to his shoulders.

The Owda – The holy mother of the Kilgari nomads whose ability to summon water preserves her people.

Rilann Blake – An extremely attractive dark-haired, blue-eyed spy for King Oro Develen of Castabal.

Finngill "Finn" Skellig – A boy of the race known as Selkans, which are seal-like in nature. He is an expert swimmer, diver, and sailor, as are all Selkans, but he eschews ship life. Hit with a boom on his first day out to sea, he was knocked unconscious and fell overboard in rough weather and only survived by being immediately rescued by seals. He is a bit of a misfit and outcast because he chooses to stay in Sessirra. He is short in stature and has a rounded body that belays his strength and agility. Like all Selkans, his skin is the color of wet sand and his hair light like dry beach sand. He is friendly and good-natured and makes close friends with Greylin.

Animals:
Bane – A large Midnight Friesen heartbound to Reist D'Arcannon. His full name is Cobalt's Darkest Bane sired by Cobalt's Midnight Thunderstrike to Tahvatar's Regal Star. Like all horses bred for Mazarine warriors, his coat is a deep blue black. He is a formidible fighter and a lot to handle.

Brekke – A wolfhound that lives in the wild but is fond of Reist D'Arcannon and accompanies him when they are far from towns, which he detests. He appears and retreats at will.

Merelda – A beautiful white mare heartbound to Heron Hollinghast. She is mostly Rabbina with some Castabalian blood, so she is taller than most Rabbinas, which is good because Hollinghast is very tall and would look silly on smaller horses. She is smart and understands much of human speech.

Roki – An unusual mount called a Fells Horse, Fells Pony or Leopard Horse depending on the regional dialect. He was in Kilgari lands where they called him Röyhkeä Varas meaning "bold thief" because he would steal their horses. He became heartbound to Greylin, and she shortened his name to Roki. His coat is like that of a snow leopard in the sunlight, darker in the shade, and he has cloven hooves.

Appendix IV
The Orders and Their Colors

Verses from The Covenant:

Four Great Orders I give you to guide the way from
darkness to Light,
White for the North, Red for the east, Green for the south,
and Blue for the west.

FIRST shall be the Mages of White, the bearers of
LIGHT of TRUTH to guide you through the darkness,
The LUMERIAN Order, the VALKOINEN who shall
Know The TRUTH, Preserve The TRUTH, and Discover
ever anew the TRUTH of ELIEL, and in speaking the
TRUTH will not go astray.

The SECOND shall be the Servants of ELIEL, the
VERENNEN, of the Order VERMILION who will serve
the Body of ELIEL as it is manifest in the masses of the
people.
Theirs are the Sacraments and the ways of Worship.

The THIRD shall be the SURRONEN, the Healers of
ELIEL, the Order VIRIDIAN who will care for the ill
and injured and ever learn the ways of Healing.
They must ease suffering in whatever form it may take.

The FOURTH shall be the Order MAZARINE, ELIEL's
Right Hand, the PALONEN, who will keep chaos at bay,
protect the people and defend the LIGHT.
Woe to any who challenge their might for theirs will be
the strength of ELIEL.

The rest are the merchants, the tradesmen and farmers, all
those who build and work
And make the world of the people in its everyday
struggle to live in the flesh,

To them shall be all manner of colors excepting those of the Great Four who are pledged to serve them and be served by them.

Color distinctions within the Orders:
Ranked high to low

Lumerians - Master of the Covenant
Mage: White
Singer: Off-white
Acolyte: light gray
Page: dark gray

Verennen: Keepers of the Covenant
Cannons and Archcanon: Bright Red
Priests: Cherry Red
Friar: Cranberry
Pages: Copper

Surronen: Healers of the covenant
Healers: Dark Green
Counselors: True Green
Nurses: Light Green
Caregivers: Lime green

Mazarines - Protectors of the Covenant
Paladin: Midnight Blue
Knight: Dark True Blue
Warrior: Gray Blue
Squire: Cadet Blue

Appendix V

Precepts of the Covenant

Treat others as you can best assess how they would most want to be treated, but do not flatter the vain.
Think of others with forbearance, just as you would wish them to think of you.
Be just, honest, and brave.
Defend others from evil, the unjust, and the dishonest.
Practice restraint from excess in all things.
Free yourself from envy and greed for that is the path of darkness.
Forgive yourself for failing the precepts and start again.
Forgive those who fail the precepts and allow them to start again.
All evil pays the price, all goodness is blessed. That is the the working of the Law.
The Law may seem exceedingly slow, but therein lies perfection. Have faith in its working.

The litany against fear and pain is given to sustain you:

I stand as one with ELIEL, between the EL Within and the EL Without, the Above and Below, between the Darkness and the Light. Nothing can hurt me. ELIEL protects me, ELIEL defends me, ELIEL preserves my spirit. Here in the Now, there is no Place where EL is not. I shall not fear, I shall not despair. I AM EL. I am Safe. I am Eternal. Only Love will Prevail

Acknowledgements

I would once again like to thank Petra Haatainen of Oulu, Finland, for her selfless, painstaking, proofing expertise in Finnish and English that brought precise translation to the entire series. Also to Sandi Matuschka for her assistance in proofreading and line editing. Most of all, thank you to my readers whose enthusiasm for Greylin's saga fills me with joy.

A percentage of all profits are split between two charities:

Dare to Dream Ranch – a non-profit military retreat providing multi-faceted equine therapy programs primarily for those experiencing PTSD.
http://www.daretodreamranch.org

Sweet Binks Rescue, Inc. – a non-profit Wildlife Rehabilitation center
http://www.sweetbinks.org

Chapter 1

HILDE CASTLE

The SECOND shall be the Servants of ELIEL,
the Verennen, of the Order Vermilion who
will serve the Body of ELIEL as it is manifest
in the masses of the people.   Theirs are the
sacraments and the ways of worship.

-THE ORDERS OF THE COVENANT
BY ST. RAUNA

The throne room was three stories tall and half as wide, separated with fluted columns dividing it into three long sections leading to the throne, the center aisle being the widest. Tall windows adorned with gold and black hangings were on each outside wall to the right and left, and above each of them were stained glass squares depicting scenes from the life of St. Rauna. At the far end was an elevated throne with the Hilde crest woven in tapestry behind it. At least a hundred people stood in small groups in the narrower aisles, arranged in a similar way to the transepts of a church to each side of the center nave. They eyed the newcomers with critical assessment.

Off to the left of the throne a plainbard, a nonmagical singer, in black and gold livery played a kantele. It was a day of audience, judgments, and general business with petitions being put forward. All of the petitioners had been swiftly swept to the sides the room when news of the adventurers' arrival was rushed to the throne. There was a hushed sound of whispers and echoing low-voiced discussions.

At long last, Greylin thought, *here is my father, King Sterren Hilde. He doesn't look anything like I expected. Round and brown* sprang to her mind. His hair was cut straight across, level with his eyebrows in front, and even with his chin all around the sides and back. *That's a very priestly haircut for a king,* she mused. He was dressed in bright red which confused her further; she thought only priests were able to wear red.

She had traveled from Castabal, proud and confident from succeeding in the battle against the Jonji war. All that seemed to drain away as they entered New Saar and as she approached the throne, she felt shy and awkward. All that had transpired, from the discovery of the Eversilver Sword and slaying the Oarman with it, bonding with the Leopard Horse, finding the Crown of the Crescent Moon, to the recent battles fighting hundreds of Jonjishalan on the shores of Castabal—all that had made her feel capable, strong, and knowledgeable—and now her confidence seemed to vanish like a fine mist in the sun. She would sooner face a hundred Jonji than embarrass herself at this moment.

"Jaarven Hilde!" Hollinghast said. "What are you doing on the throne of Taivasta? Has something happened to the king?"

Jaarven! Greylin gasped in surprise. *That's Jaarven? That's not my father!* She felt a wave of relief for she hadn't liked the look of him at all. She noticed a hint of cold anger cross Jaarven's face at Hollinghast's challenge. It was quickly covered by a feigned graciousness.

"Alas, yes, I'm afraid the king has taken ill. The Healers have restricted him to his bed chamber. Who is this you have brought with you?"

As if he didn't know, Greylin thought. *He's only tried to kill me twice with slinkhounds.*

"My Lord Archcanon," Hollinghast replied in his silkiest voice. "I present the Princess Cianalas, who has come many miles and through much hardship to return to her rightful place."

Greylin remembered to curtsy, feeling awkward and stupid. *I should have practiced this, my horse could do it better.*

"Welcome, my child," Jaarven responded, gesturing with his hand that she approach. She took a few steps forward, warily, wishing she had never entered the castle. The man made her feel slimy.

"So," the Archcanon, continued superciliously, "Sir Heron Hollinghast, Master Mage, and the Paladin Reist D'Arcannon," he nodded, smiling at the big warrior who waited quietly. "I assume you can provide the proper proofs of her identity? And if so, can you explain why it has taken so long to bring her here? And you can further explain how she was taken from the protection of the Kingsguard?"

Oh here it comes, she thought, *this isn't going well at all.*

Hollinghast flushed, "My Lord, we found the child with the nurse Sarra Duplessy who you will remember was also nurse to—to—the former queen. She had been taken there and hidden in safety. She wears the rings given to her by her mother."

Greylin lifted her hand, and the rings sparkled in the light. This startled the Archcanon but he recovered quickly, "So, that's where they went. We thought they had been stolen. Tell me, child, what have you been doing all this time?"

He didn't know about the rings, she thought. *He was hoping I had no proof.* She opened her mouth to answer, but nothing came out. The healers had warned her that their cure was not completely reliable. Her voice could come and go the rest of her life. Standing there, dumb and silent, she felt ignorant, rough, and common, as though if she did speak, her accent was something to be laughed at, her manners atrocious. Her mind went blank, and she tried again, but could make no sound. *Oh why now?* She felt panicky and her eyes darted down and to her right and left as she tried to collect herself. She noticed then that the kantele plainbard was looking at her and smirking. *He's doing this,* she thought. *He's making magic to undermine me. He's not a mage and shouldn't be allowed to do that!*

Hollinghast, coming to the same conclusion, jumped in and explained her exploits over the past few months. Partway through the story he plucked a chord on his kantelyre and string broke on the kantele in the corner. The plainbard jumped back as though he had been stung.

"I see," said the Archcanon in a way that expressed that he didn't believe any of it. "And what did you do before then?" he asked turning to Greylin once more.

"D-d-daaaaara and I ran a fa-fa-a-rm together," she managed to croak. "We raised sheep for wool and crops for ourselves as well as some chickens and p-pi-pigs," she stuttered and stammered, but she thought, *at least my voice is coming back.*

The people were now drawing closer behind and to the sides of them, eager to listen to what was transpiring. Greylin could feel their stares and couldn't help glancing at their rich clothes and garish faces painted with rouges and dark pencil. When she said "pigs" there was a definite titter from the crowd, someone in the back laughed. *Why did I say that?* she thought. *We only raised pigs one year! What is coming out of my mouth!*

"Daara?" Jaarven's voice was dripping with scorn. "Is this her?" he asked, nodding and gesturing at Rilah.

"No, no, this is the Lady Rilah, sister to Lord Rilann of Castabal and granted leave to accompany her friend and companion." This for some reason caused murmuring though Greylin had no inking why. If Rilah was surprised that she and Rilann had somehow been advanced to "Lord" and "Lady" she gave no sign except for a slight raising of her chin.

"Sarra called herself 'Daara', presumably as an alias." Hollinghast answered, steering the conversation away.

"Yes, a farm, well," Jaarven said. "You'll have to tell me more about the pigs another time." A wave of tittering issued from the crowd. "Now I think we need to find you suitable rooms and all that. I need to talk to the Master Mage…and you also, Paladin, I believe you also had a hand in keeping the king's daughter from him. It seems he will always be plagued by your family. Young lady, you may take your leave with your friend." He gestured to the back of the room.

Greylin looked over in alarm at Hollinghast and D'Arcannon. What had she expected? That they wouldn't be separated? She and Rilah turned reluctantly and were escorted away by the palace guard. Greylin turned to catch one last desperate look at Hollinghast and D'Arcannon. She realized with crushing finality that their traveling days were over. She might never see them again except from a distance, and that only if she were lucky. She had come to trust them both and now— just like that—she was abruptly torn away. As they left the throne room, a woman approached.

"Welcome, both of you," she said graciously, "I am Queen Lyda, I'll take you up." She turned to the guard, "You're relieved,"

The two men ordered to accompany them looked momentarily confused, but they weren't going to go against the queen's order.

Lyda led them down a corridor and up two flights of marble stairs. Lyda was as kind and gracious as Jaarven had been formidable, chattering pleasantly as she led them along corridors of marble and stone. She was brown-haired and blue-eyed, not beautiful but pleasant, and they both liked her immediately. Their fears were allayed and Greylin resisted the urge to make a run for it.

Large windows ran the length of the corridors on the outside wall of the second floor. They were curtained in the colors of the four great Orders: red, white, green, and blue. Tapestries on the walls on the inner side predominated in the same colors, as did elaborately woven rugs. The colors of the orders were everywhere, and Greylin realized that New Saar was the heart of the Covenant of St. Rauna. It represented all of Allanda, its orders and colors. Only those private rooms, clothes, and personal belongings bore the yellow-gold and black hues of the House of Hilde.

"Let's see, where should we put you?" Queen Lyda chattered on. "Oh, I know, perhaps in your mother's old room. It was lovely and hasn't been used," she said gaily and threw open the door.

It was indeed a lovely room; it was paneled in ladywood with pink and pale green diamond-paned windows. Greylin's eyes were drawn to a discreet panel door in a far corner. She walked over to it, touched it, and pulled it open.

"They say that's the way your nurse took you," the queen said. "It is interesting that you would find it right away. Your disappearance was always a mystery. We wondered if you'd gone that way but no one saw you on the other end. No one ever knew for sure. The two guards who were at the door that day were executed. It was thought that they had to have cooperated with your disappearance."

Greylin looked at her in horror, "But they had nothing to do with it!" A wave of guilt washed over her. She knew it wasn't her fault, not her decision or action that resulted in their deaths, but she still felt somehow responsible by being the reason for their deaths. *What kind of place have I come to?*

Then, to her horror, she saw a ghost crossing to the window, her mother's wraith clawing at the casement! The shade of Queen Isabela went through the motions of opening the window, looking out in horror, then turning to walk away, sobbing. She disappeared, then appeared again! There she was at the window once more, opening it, looking in horror, then turning away.

Greylin felt all the color drain from her face and she stood rooted to the floor. Isabela was beautiful, but to see her like this was a terrible thing. As Greylin stood transfixed, watching it play over and over, the apparition suddenly stopped and looked at her. It seemed to thicken as though there were two of them, one inside the other, and then, glaring, she said, "I am not here" in a low voice that horrified Greylin.

Queen Lyda stopped her chatter when she saw the color drain from Greylin's face. She took her arm and led her out of the room. Obviously, she could see nothing. Rilah was looking at Greylin in puzzlement as well. They might not understand, but they could tell she was shaken.

"Well, maybe not this one," Lyda said. "That might not have been the wisest choice on my part after all. I don't know what I was thinking. I know! Your grandmother's room. I'll have them come freshen it up. It's on the other side of the castle. Less drafty and no view of the Tower. Your grandmother, that was Rosalba, you know, she liked her comforts, and it was a warm room I think, on this side. Nice in the winter. Here you go."

This room held no horrors, at least none that Greylin could see. There was a lingering sense of watchfulness, though, but it was a welcoming one. It was a room Greylin and Rilah liked immediately because it was a double room, the one next to it a twin of the first and linked by a common door, perfect for both of them. The patterns here were warm and relaxed, mostly russet and golds, olives and browns. A fireplace framed in dark wood faced the bed, two stuffed chairs on either side. Bookcases lined the walls and tall windows with padded window seats gave light for reading. The beds were wide with lovely canopies and hangings all around. To one side of the bed the wall opened up to a large closet, some of which still held clothing.

"Oh, look at this!" Lyda said. "I had no idea all this was in here. Well, that won't do, we'll have to get you suited up right away. We'll have to call in Jules and Echo for an emergency fitting tomorrow. I think you'd like dinner in your rooms tonight, yes?"

"Yes, oh yes, please. I would be most grateful." Greylin replied. She really wasn't ready to face Jaarven again, or anyone.

"Well, good, then we can get you presentable tomorrow."

Presentable? Are we not presentable? She should have seen me a few days ago.

"Wait!" Greylin said as the queen was about to leave. "Is it possible to see the king?"

"Oh well," Lyda looked down and pursed her lips. "I don't know. You see it's not up to me. I will ask the Healers for you."

If you would like to know more about

The Chalice Rose Series, please visit

https://cksholly/home/blog/

or go to

fb.me/CKSholly

Made in United States
North Haven, CT
26 November 2021

11515446R00129